Nine
Fairy
Tales

Capek, Karel, 1890-
1938.

Nine fairy tales

$24.95

DATE			

Nine Fairy Tales
by Karel Čapek

and

One More

Thrown in

for Good

Measure

Translated by Dagmar Herrmann

With Illustrations by Josef Čapek

Northwestern University Press
Evanston, Illinois

Northwestern University Press
Evanston, Illinois 60201

First published as *Devatero pohádek a ještě jedna od Josefa Čapka jako přívažek* by Fr. Borový—Aventinum, Prague, 1932. English translation © 1990 by Dagmar Herrmann. Published 1990 by Northwestern University Press. All rights reserved.

Library of Congress Cataloging-in-Publication Data

Čapek, Karel, 1890–1938.
  [Devatero pohádek a ještě jedna přívažek od Josefa Čapka. English]
  Nine fairy tales by Karel Čapek ; and one more thrown in for good measure / Karel Čapek ; translated by Dagmar Herrmann ; with illustrations by Josef Čapek.
      p.   cm.
  Translation of : Devatero pohádek a ještě jedna přívažek od Josefa Čapka.
  ISBN 0-8101-0864-X. — ISBN 0-8101-0865-8 (pbk.)
  1. Tales—Czechoslovakia.   I. Title.
PZ70.C9C26   1990

                                                    90-33618
                                                    CIP

Contents

The
Great
Cat's
Tale

How the King Bought a Cat

I n the Land of Pranksters there reigned a king about whom it could be said that he ruled happily. All his subjects, since they had to, obeyed him with pleasure and love. Only his daughter, the little princess, sometimes did not.

The king, you see, had asked her not to play ball on the steps of the palace, but she would not listen. The moment her nanny took a short nap, she began running up the steps holding her ball. Well, just there and then, whether it was the Lord who punished her or the Devil who tripped her, she fell and skinned her knee. She sat down on the steps and cried—had she not been a princess, I would have said that she yelled her head off. Needless to say, ladies-in-waiting with washbowls of crystal and bandages of silk, ten court physicians, and three court chaplains immediately assembled, but no one could rid the princess of her pain.

Just then, an old woman came trudging by. Seeing the princess crying on the steps, she knelt down beside her and said kindly, "Don't cry, Princess. If I brought you an animal with eyes like emeralds which no one could steal, with whiskers all the way out to here but not those of a man, with fur that crackles yet does not burn, with paws of silk that never wear thin, with sixteen knives in their tiny pouches but none that are used with forks, you wouldn't cry anymore, would you?"

The princess looked at the old woman. One of the girl's blue eyes still shed tears though the other was already smiling. "But Granny," she said, "there isn't a creature like that in the whole world!" "But there is," the grandma said. "If His Majesty the King were to give me what I ask for, I'd bring the animal to you straight away!" Having said this, she slowly hobbled off.

The princess still sat on the steps, but she was not crying anymore, just wondering what animal the granny had meant. Before long, she started to feel sorry that she did not have the animal and that the old woman was not going to bring her anything, so again, she began to weep. His Majesty the King had seen and heard everything, for he had watched from the window to learn why the princess had been carrying on so much. Having noticed how nicely the old woman had calmed the princess, he returned to his throne among his ministers and counselors, but he couldn't get that animal out of his mind. "It has eyes like emeralds," he kept repeating to himself, "yet no one can steal them; whiskers all the way out to here but not those of a man; fur that crackles yet does not burn; paws of silk that never wear thin; sixteen knives in their tiny pouches but none that are used with forks. What can it be?" The ministers observed the king mumbling, shaking his head, and gesturing with his hands as if fashioning an enormous mustache under his nose. It was then that the old chancellor asked him just *what* he was doing.

"I am thinking about an animal," said the king, "with eyes like emeralds that no one can steal, with whiskers all the way out to here but not those of a man, with fur that crackles yet does not burn, with paws of silk that never wear thin, with sixteen knives in their tiny pouches but none that are used with a fork to cut meat. Would you know what animal that is?"

Now it was the ministers and counselors who shook their heads and fashioned enormous mustaches in the air under their noses, but not one could figure out what animal it was. Finally, the old chancellor spoke. He used the very words of the princess when she had spoken to the old woman. "But there isn't a creature like that in the whole world, Your Majesty."

The king, however, refused to hear of it and dispatched his fastest courier in search of the old woman. Speeding on his horse, flying until sparks shot up from beneath its hooves, the courier came upon the old woman sitting in front of her cottage. "Grandma," the courier cried from his saddle, "His Majesty the King *must* have that animal."

"His Majesty will have what he wants," answered the old woman, "if he gives me as many silver coins as the finest ones of silver that fit under his mother's bonnet."

The courier rushed back to the palace, the dust rising to the sky. "Your Majesty," he announced, "Granny will bring you the animal if you give her as many silver coins as the finest ones of silver that fit under your mother's bonnet."

"That won't be much," the king thought, and swore to himself with a great oath that he would give the old woman exactly that many coins and no more. Then he ran right off to his mother. "Mama," he said, "we are to receive a visitor. Why don't you put on that nice little bonnet of yours, you know, the tiniest of them all, the one that covers only a lock of your hair?" And his old mother agreed.

So the granny came to the palace, and on her back she carried a basket neatly tied with a scarf. In the large hall, the king, the Queen Mother, and the princess were waiting expectantly. So were all the ministers, counselors, generals, and dignitaries, so curious they were breathless. Little by little the old woman untied the scarf. The king descended from his throne to inspect the animal. At last, as the old woman pulled away the scarf, a black cat leaped from the basket and with a single bound sat down on the throne.

"But Granny," the king cried in disappointment, "you must be joking! This is only a cat!"

The old woman put her hands on her hips. "Joking? Just look," she said and pointed to the cat. As the cat stretched out upon the throne, its eyes shone bright green like the most beautiful emeralds. "Just look," said the old woman, "doesn't it have emerald eyes? And these, Your Majesty, no one can steal. And it has whiskers, too, though not those of a man."

"But," protested the king, "its coat is dark, it doesn't crackle."

"Just you wait," the old woman objected, and began stroking the fur against the grain. The crackling sounds of small electric sparks filled the air. "And it has silken paws," continued the old woman. "Even a young princess, if she ran barefoot on her tiptoes, could not run more quietly."

"Well, all right," the king admitted. "But a cat has not even one little pouch, and where are the sixteen knives?"

"Those silken paws have pouches," said the old woman, "and in each of them is a sharp knife—a tiny claw."

At that point, the king ordered the old chancellor to count the cat's claws. When the chancellor bent toward the cat and grabbed its foot—to count—the animal hissed and struck him near the eye.

The chancellor straightened, covering his eye, and said, "Your Majesty, my vision is weak but I do believe there are many claws in that paw. I am quite sure of four."

So the king commanded his first footman to count the cat's claws. The footman grabbed the cat but straightened at once, all red in the face. Touching his injured nose, he said, "Twelve, Your Majesty. I've just counted another eight, four on each side."

Then the king pointed to his highest dignitary to continue counting, but no sooner had that venerable gentleman bent to the cat, than he straightened up again, stroking his beard, and said, "There are exactly sixteen claws, Your Majesty; I've just counted the last four."

"Well, do I have a choice?" sighed the king. "It looks like I'll have to buy that cat. But you've sure played a trick on me, Grandma, I'll say that."

So the king could do nothing but plunk down the silver coins. He removed the tiny bonnet, the tiniest of them all, from his mother's head and placed it over the coins. The bonnet was so small it hardly covered five.

"Here, Granny, you've got your silver coins. Farewell, now," said the king, happy that he had escaped so cheaply.

But the old woman just shook her head and said, "That wasn't the agreement, Your Majesty. Your Majesty was to give me as many coins as the finest silver that could fit under your mother's bonnet."

"Can't you see," protested the king, "that no more than five coins of the finest silver can fit beneath that bonnet?"

The old woman took the bonnet in her hands. Stroking it and turning it in her palm, she said slowly, "I believe that the finest silver in the world is your mother's silver hair."

The king looked at the old woman, then at his mother, and said softly, "You are right, old woman."

The old woman put the little bonnet back on the head of the Queen Mother. She caressed the silvery hair and said, "And now, Your Majesty will give me as many coins as there are hairs beneath your mother's bonnet."

The king marveled, the king frowned, and, finally, the king smiled. "Grandma," he said, "you really are a prankster from the Land of Pranksters."

But, children, a promise is a promise, so the king had to pay the woman what she requested. He asked his mother to sit down and ordered the chief accountant to count the silver hairs which fit under her bonnet. The accountant proceeded to count—and he kept on counting. The king's mother held still, not moving a bit, and soon . . . you know . . . how old people like their sleep, the Queen Mother dozed off.

While she slept, the accountant counted hair after hair and just when he had counted to one thousand—perhaps he had pulled too much on a silver hair—the king's mother awoke.

"Alas," she cried out, "why did you wake me up? I was having a lively dream: I dreamed that the future king had just crossed our country's border."

The old granny was startled. "That's strange," she blurted out, "my grandson was to move in with me only today from the neighboring country."

The king did not hear a word she said, for he was shouting, "Where, Mama, from which royal house comes the future king?"

"That I do not know," said his mother. "You awakened me too soon."

Meanwhile, the chief accountant continued counting. Soon, the king's mother fell asleep again. The accountant kept counting and counting until he reached two thousand when, again, his hand quivered and he tugged too hard on a silver hair.

"What is it, children?" cried the king's mother. "Why do you rouse me again? Just now, I was dreaming that the black cat would bring us the future king."

"Come now, Mama," the king said doubtfully. "Whoever heard of a cat bringing a person home?"

"Well, that's what I dreamed," said the Queen Mother. "And now, just let me sleep."

Again, the king's mother fell asleep and, again, the accountant counted. When he had counted the three thousandth hair—to the very last one—his hand shook and, for the third time, he pulled too hard.

"How disrespectful you are, the lot of you," cried the king's mother. "Can't you let an old woman sleep a little? Just now, I dreamed that the future king was arriving with his entire house."

"Now, Mother, I beg you," the king protested, "that couldn't possibly be true. Who could arrive with an entire royal palace?"

"Do not waste words, son," his mother reproached him. "One never knows what the future may bring."

"That's right," nodded the old granny, "your old mother is correct, Your Majesty. My husband, saints preserve him, had his future read by a Gypsy woman. 'One day,' she told him, 'a rooster will peck up your whole farm.' Poor man, he laughed and said, 'You know, Gypsy woman, that could never be.' Just like you, Your Majesty."

"But it wasn't true, was it?" asked the king eagerly.

The old woman wiped her eyes. "Well then. One day, a red rooster swept in like a fireball and pecked up everything in sight. Afterward, the man just walked around as if bereft of his senses, saying over and over, 'The Gypsy woman was right! The Gypsy woman was right!' It has been twenty years now since he met his maker, poor man."

The old woman burst into fresh tears, at which point the Queen Mother threw her arms around the woman's neck and, stroking her face, said, "Do not cry, Granny, or I will too." The king became frightened and began jingling the silver coins. Quickly, he plunked one coin after another on the table until he had laid out all three thousand, as many as the silver hairs covered by the Queen Mother's bonnet. "Here, Granny," he said, "here, this is yours. And God bless you. I'll never save a penny with you, that's for sure."

The old woman smiled and everyone smiled with her as she stuffed her purse with coins. If only the purse had been large enough! She had to shovel the coins into the basket, and the basket became so full she couldn't even lift it. Two of the generals and the king himself helped her raise the basket onto her back. Then the old woman bowed to everybody and bid farewell to the king's mother. She looked around for Youra, her black cat, but Youra was nowhere in sight. All the granny's turning and calling, "Here, kitty kitty, here, kitty kitty" was to no avail. Then somebody's little feet sticking out from behind the throne caught her eye. The old woman tiptoed over. What did she see but the princess, who had fallen asleep in the nook behind the throne. And in her lap, sleeping and purring, was precious Youra.

So, the woman took a coin from her pocket and placed it in the palm of the princess. If it was the granny's wish that the coin be kept as a keepsake, she made a great mistake. For when the princess awoke and found the cat in her lap and a coin in her hand, she took the cat into her arms and very quickly spent the money on candy. Even all that, however, the old woman may have known well beforehand.

While the princess slept, the old woman returned home, pleased at having earned so much money and content to leave Youra in such good hands. What made her

happiest, though, was that just then the coachman arrived
with Vašek, her grandson.

All the Tricks a Cat Can Pull

By now, you know that the cat's name was Youra. She had many nicknames, though. The princess called her "Kitty," "Kittycat," "Kitten," "Pussy," "Pussycat," "Licker," and "Smokey," which only shows you how much she liked her. Each morning as soon as the princess opened her eyes, she could see the kitten lounging on the goosedown quilt, purring, just pretending to be doing something. They washed themselves together. (The cat much more thoroughly, of course, though with only her paw and tongue; she also remained clean much longer than the princess, who got herself thoroughly and completely dirty, as only children can.)

At the same time, Youra was a cat like every other, though she liked to sit and doze on the royal throne, something other cats usually cannot do. Perhaps she was thinking of the lion, her uncle many times removed and king of all the animals. Or perhaps it just seemed as if she were reminiscing, for a mouse had merely to edge from its hole and with one leap Youra would catch it and place it at the foot of the throne, no matter if the largest and most illustrious assembly were present.

One day, the king had to settle a dispute between two venerable gentlemen. Both stood before the steps of the throne, quarreling, to no end, about who was in the right. At the height of the argument, Youra appeared, placed a dead mouse on the floor, and proudly awaited recognition. One of the gentlemen did not even notice, but the other bent down right away and patted her. "Aha," the king said to himself instantly, "this is a righteous man; he gives credit where credit is due." And he turned out to be right, of course.

The king kept two dogs in his palace, one called Buffo, the other Buffino. When they first noticed Youra dozing in the front yard, they exchanged glances, as if to say, "Listen, my friend, this one is not our countryman." And, as if agreed to beforehand, they attacked. The cat just backed up to the wall and bristled, her tail as thick as a broom. Had Buffo and Buffino been smarter, they would have known what her arched back meant. But since they were stupid, they wanted only to sniff her. When Buffo approached, he got hit so hard on his muzzle he yelped, lowered his tail, and ran away so fast it took him an hour to stop. For two days afterward, he shook with fright.

Seeing this, Buffino was a little alarmed but decided to play hero. "Listen, you misfit," he told Youra, "don't you start with me. When I bark, even the moon in the sky is frightened." To prove it, he barked so loudly that all the windowpanes for a mile around cracked.

Youra didn't even blink, and when Buffino stopped barking, she said, "You indeed know a little about yelping, but when I hiss even a snake's blood turns cold with fear." To prove it, she produced a hiss so piercing that every one of Buffino's hairs bristled with terror.

After pulling himself together, he started anew. "Big deal! Hissing has never been considered heroic. You just watch me run!" Indeed, before the cat could utter a word, Buffino ran around the palace so fast that even the palace's turret started spinning.

Youra pretended not to be at all impressed, though she was a bit bewildered. "Well," she said, "now at least I know how fast you'll run from me. You watch *this*. If someone a hundred thousand times stronger than you tries to get me, I'd run *this* fast." And with three leaps, Youra was on a treetop—so high Buffino got terribly dizzy when he looked at her.

Then he pulled himself together, and said, "You know, of course, that a decent dog does not climb trees. If you wish to learn what I can really do, then listen. I need only to sniff and snuff and I already know that in the neighboring kingdom the queen is roasting quail for dinner and that we'll be dining on roast goose."

Secretly, the cat tried to snuff, but she couldn't smell a thing. She was immensely impressed with the dog's extraordinary sense of smell, but appeared quite unperturbed. "That's nothing compared with my hearing," she said. "Right now, for instance, I hear the needle our queen just dropped as well as the bells in the neighboring kingdom, which will chime noon in fifteen minutes."

Awestruck, but unwilling to surrender, Buffino said, "Let me tell you something. Let's not snarl at each other anymore. Don't be afraid of me and come down from the tree."

"I am not scared of you at all," Youra said, "but I have a different proposal. Don't you be afraid of me and come up here, in the tree."

"I shall climb up right away, but first—wag your tail, like we dogs do." And he wagged his tail till it wiggled.

Youra tried to do the same but somehow just couldn't. (How could she, when God had taught only dogs how to do it?) Nevertheless, not to appear a coward, she climbed down and came close to Buffino. "We cats," she said, "when we are not plotting something evil, purr like this. Could you try it a little, out of friendship?"

Buffino tried, but to no avail. All he could do was emit such a growl that he himself was ashamed. "Let's go," he said quickly, "let's go barking at people instead. That's much more fun!"

"I know I wouldn't be able to bark," Youra objected modestly, "but we could climb to the edge of the roof and enjoy the view, if you care to."

"Forgive me, I cannot," said Buffino in embarrassment. "Such height somehow always makes me dizzy. But we could go rabbit hunting together. That would definitely be much better."

"I couldn't possibly hunt for rabbits," the cat said. "My legs were not made for it. But if you cared to join me, I'd lead you to a tree where we could hunt for birds."

Buffino reflected sadly. "Well, Youra," he said finally, "I'm afraid that won't do either. I have a suggestion, though. I will stay the way I am, a dog in the woods and in the streets, and you stay the way you are, a cat in the trees and on the rooftops. But here, in the palace—in the palace yard and in the palace garden—let's forget about cats and dogs and just be friends."

And so it was. They became so used to each other that they began copying one another's ways. Youra learned to run after the princess like a dog, and Buffino, seeing the cat bringing dead mice to the king, triumphantly brought him bones he had dug up from the trash or had found in the street. (It should be mentioned, though, that he did not earn as much praise for his feat as the cat for hers.)

Late one night, asleep in his doghouse (you no doubt realize, children, that a royal doghouse is built of cedar and mahogany), Buffino dreamed of seeing a rabbit. He chased it so fast that his paws jerked in sleep. He felt a tap on his muzzle. "Hey," he started, "what's going on?"

"Hush," whispered a familiar voice, "can't you be a little quiet?" It was Youra; she looked darker than the night itself, except that her green eyes shone with intelligence and excitement. "I was sitting on the rooftop," Youra whispered, "thinking of all kind of things, the way I always do when—you know how well I hear—I heard somebody's steps far away in the royal garden."

"Ruff," Buffino barked.

"Hush," hissed Youra. "I bet it's a thief! And guess what! We are going to catch him!"

"Right," barked the dog eagerly, "right! I'm already on my way." So together they left for the garden.

The night was pitch black. Buffino wanted to take the lead but became confused in the dark and tripped at each step. "Youra," he whispered anxiously. "Youra, I can't see a thing."

"I see at night as well as in daylight," said Youra. "Let me go first. You sniff and follow."

And so it was.

"Here, I've got it," Buffino cried suddenly. "I'm on somebody's track." His muzzle almost to the ground, he followed the trail as if he could see it. And it was Youra now who followed. "Pssst," she whispered after a while, "I can see him. There he is, right in front of you."

"Halt!" shouted Buffino in a powerful voice. "Get, get, get him! Overpower him! Hey, buddy! Hey, you hoodlum! Hey, you villain! Hey, you clumsy giant! Choke him, tramp him, smear him, thrash him, roll up your sleeves and tear him up! Ha-ha-ha!"

Hearing all that, the thief got so scared he began to run. Buffino chased him, bit him on the calf, tore his trousers, jumped under his feet, and tripped him. To top it all, he bit him on the ear. Frightened and hardly able to get up or pull himself away, the thief just managed to clamber up a tree. Now it was Youra's turn. She dashed after him, jumped on his neck, and kept scratching and biting, scratching and smiting, as hard as she could. "Pfff," she sputtered and fizzled, "I'll cure you like a ham, you'll ha-a-ang. I'll k-k-i-i-ll you, I'll c-c-c-ut you up, I'll m-m-angle you all to pieces!"

"Ha," yelled Buffino from below, "mob him, whack him, slaughter him, knock him down, throw him down to me, slay him, bump him, tie him up, bite him and don't let go!"

"I give up," the thief howled in mortal anguish, falling from the tree like a pear. He knelt down, raised both hands toward the sky, and begged: "Don't kill me, I beseech you, I'm giving myself up! Take me wherever you want, for heaven's sake!"

And so they set out for the palace: Youra led, her tail raised like a saber, followed by the thief with raised hands, Buffino marching in the rear. Halfway there, they were met by sentries carrying lanterns who had been awakened by the noise. They too joined the procession. With pomp and ceremony, Youra and Buffino brought the

thief to the palace. The king himself and the queen too had arisen and were watching everything from the window. Only the princess slept through it all. Perhaps she would have slept through breakfast as well had it not been for Youra who, as she did each morning, came to primp herself on the princess's feather bed with such a sweet expression on her face that one might have thought nothing at all had happened the night before.

Youra could, of course, do many more and different things but if we listed them all, this story would never come to an end. Let me just tell you a few of her feats:

Sometimes she would catch fish from a brook with her paw.

She also ate cucumber salad.

With the innocent expression of an angel, she would also catch birds, although she had been told it was strictly forbidden.

She would play so nicely that one could watch her all day long.

Should you wish to find out more about Youra, you need only lovingly observe any other cat. Every cat resembles Youra a little and each knows thousands of nice and funny tricks she won't conceal from anyone who will not harm her.

How the Detectives Chased the Magician

Talking about the tricks a cat can pull, I must tell you something else as well. Somehow, somewhere the princess heard from someone that no matter how far a kitten falls, it won't get hurt, for it will always land safely on its feet. So one day, the princess carried Youra up to the palace attic and, just to see for herself, she tossed Youra out a small window. Then, quickly, she peeked out to see if her kitten had really landed on her feet. Well, Youra didn't. Her fall ended on the head of a gentleman who just happened to be passing in the street below. Youra either sank her claws into his head or he became displeased by something else—at any rate, the man didn't let Youra sit on his head as the princess might have thought he should have. He snatched her off, hid her under his cloak, and disappeared.

The princess ran from the attic straight to her father, the king. "Boo-hoo," she sobbed, "A man walked under our windows and he stole our You—Youra!"

When His Majesty heard this, he thought to himself, "A cat here, a cat there, who gives a fig about cats." "But this one is supposed to bring us the future king," he remembered uneasily. "This one I'd rather not lose."

Right away, His Majesty called for the police chief. "Listen," he said. "Someone stole Youra, our black cat. The man carried her away under his overcoat. They say he went that way, over there."

The police chief knit his brow, reflected for half an hour, and at last proclaimed, "With God's help and with the help of the metropolitan and secret police, the army and navy, the artillery, the fire brigade, all the submarines and airships, as well as fortunetellers and soothsayers, and all the rest of the population, I will find that cat, Your Majesty, so help me God!"

Immediately, he called in his best detectives. A detective, children, is a gentleman who works for the secret police. He dresses in regular clothes like any of us, but he is always in disguise so that no one can recognize him. A detective always figures out everything, finds out everything, catches up with everyone, accomplishes everything, and isn't frightened of anything. As you can see, to be a detective is not such an easy thing.

As I said, the chief immediately summoned his best detectives, three cousins, named Nosey Parker, Alec Smart, and Percy Witling; also a sly Italian, Signore Foxelli; a joyful fat Dutchman, Mynheer Rolling van Plump; a giant Slav, Bear Bulloff; and a gloomy, taciturn Scot, Mister Gruff Surly. In the blink of an eye they were apprised of the situation. They also were told that whoever found the cat would be handsomely rewarded.

"Si," cried Foxelli.

"Jaa," said Rolling joyfully.

"Mm," growled Bear Bulloff.

"Well," added Surly curtly.

The three cousins simply winked at one another.

Within fifteen minutes, Nosey Parker learned that a man with a black cat under his overcoat had been seen walking down Spálená Street.

Within half an hour, Alec Smart reported that a man with a black cat under his overcoat had been spotted in the vicinity of Vinohrady.

Within an hour, Percy Witling dashed in with news that a man with a black cat under his overcoat was sitting in a tavern in Strašnice having a beer.

Foxelli, Rolling, Bulloff, and Surly leaped into a car that was standing by and raced to Strašnice.

"Men," said Foxelli when they arrived. "A criminal as astute as this one can be apprehended only through devious means. Let me do the job," added the sly old fox, thinking only of reaping the reward for himself.

Quickly, he disguised himself as a ropemaker and, pretending to be selling ropes, headed for the tavern. Inside sat a stranger in a black suit. He had raven hair, a black mustache, and a pale face with exquisite though mirthless eyes. "That's him," the detective detected in a twinkle.

"Ahem, excuse me, sir, signore, I sell ropes, gorgeous firm ropes. They don't tear, they don't unravel, and they are as strong as iron," he twittered in broken Czech while displaying his ropes: unfolding them, drawing them out, stretching them, unwinding them, tossing them from one hand to the other while watching for the right moment to throw a noose round the stranger's hands and tie him up.

"No, thanks," said the stranger, and with his finger he scribbled something on the table.

"Just look here, mister," Foxelli jabbered even more eagerly, as he began tossing, stretching, and unwinding the ropes more rapidly. "Just look how long, how tough, how thin, how strong, how white they are, what quality, what—what—what the devil!" he screamed anxiously. "What's going on?" As he was tossing, stretching, drawing and turning the ropes, his hands mysteriously became entangled in them. The ropes themselves had formed a noose, doubling, tangling, tying, and binding him. I must be going mad, Foxelli thought, for the ropes had firmly tied him up, for good and all.

Foxelli began to sweat in fear, yet he still believed he could untangle himself. He began twisting and squirming, jolting and writhing. He jumped, bent, and twirled, trying somehow to extricate himself from those ropes, all the time chattering faster and faster, "Just look here, look at the quality, at the strength, at the firmness, length, resiliency. What beauty, what ropes, God Almighty!" And as he twisted and jumped, the ropes kept spinning around, swaddling him. Finally, quite breathless, his arms and legs laced and fettered, with ropes crisscrossing him in all directions, Signore Foxelli tottered and slumped to the floor.

The stranger sat still, not twitching an eyebrow, with his melancholy eyes fixed on the table where he scribbled with his finger.

Outside, the detectives began to wonder what was taking Foxelli so long. "Mm," Bear Bulloff growled resolutely and stormed the tavern. Lo and behold, there lay Foxelli, all trussed up, stretched on the floor, and at the table sat the stranger, his head bowed, scribbling with his finger on the tablecloth.

"Mm," snarled Bulloff.

"You were saying . . . " said the stranger.

"That I am arresting you," said Bulloff.

The stranger merely lifted his bewitching eyes.

Bulloff held up his enormous fist, ready to do battle, but when he looked into those eyes, he suddenly felt somewhat queasy. He slid his hands into his pockets and said, "I—er, well, I mean, it would be better if you surrendered voluntarily. Once I get hold of a man there isn't a single unbroken bone left in his body."

"Is that so?" said the stranger.

"And I really mean it. All I need is to tap your shoulder once, and you'll turn lame. My name's Bear Bulloff."

"Sounds nice, I'd say. Though strength isn't all, my dear fellow. And while talking to me, kindly remove your fists from your pockets, if you don't mind."

Bulloff, slightly embarrassed, wanted to pull his hands out of his pockets, but he couldn't. He tried the right—it held fast like an ingrown nail. He tried the left—it was as if a barbell held it down. Yet barbells, he was sure, he could lift, but not his own hands, no matter how hard he jerked or tugged or pulled.

"It's a bad joke," Bulloff grumbled helplessly.

"Not as bad as you think," the stranger said slowly, and kept scribbling with his finger on the table.

While Bulloff struggled and sweated and squirmed to extricate his hands from his pockets, the detectives wondered what was taking him so long.

"My turn," Rolling said curtly and, broad as he was, he rolled into the tavern. What did he see? Foxelli trussed up, stretched on the floor, Bulloff bouncing on his haunches like a bear, his hands deep in his pockets and there, sitting at a table, a stranger, his head bowed, scribbling with his finger on the tabletop.

"Coming to arrest me?" the stranger asked before Rolling could utter a word.

"At your service," cried Rolling obligingly, pulling iron handcuffs out of his pocket. "If you please, sir, you need only stretch out your delicate little hands, we'll handcuff them here with these nice cold handcuffs, brand new little handcuffs, sir, made of the finest steel, with a beautiful small wrought-iron chain, all goods of the finest quality." While reciting this, silly Rolling rattled the handcuffs, tossing them from hand to hand, as if exhibiting merchandise in a shop. "Please yourself," he went on, chattering merrily, "here, no one is coerced but we do force just a little bit those who refuse to cooperate. Look at these fine bracelets, a beautiful fit, sir; they won't squeeze, they won't pinch, with a snaplock, too." Just then Rolling's face reddened and, jiggling the handcuffs faster and faster, he began to perspire. "Gorgeous hand-hand-handcuffs, like custom made, oh heavens! of gu-uu-nm-m-metal, sir, tempered in oh-oh-oh dear me! in fire!, in the hot-t-t-test fur-fur-fu-u-rnace and—damn it!" Rolling suddenly yelled and hurled the handcuffs to the floor. What else could he have done with them? Why do you think he was constantly tossing them from one hand to the other—why, the handcuffs were glowing hot, that's why. Hitting the floor, they burned a hole in it, nearly setting the wood aflame.

And outside the tavern Surly wondered why no one was coming back. "Well," he uttered decisively, pulled out his gun, and entered the tavern. He couldn't believe his eyes. Through thick smoke he saw Rolling jumping up and down, Bulloff with his hands in his pockets, squirming, Foxelli trussed up on the floor, and a stranger sitting at a table, drumming his fingers on the tablecloth.

"Well?" Surly spoke, aiming the revolver directly at the stranger. The stranger gave him a sweet, pensive look. Facing those eyes, Surly felt his hand quiver, but overcoming his momentary indecision, he fired from the closest range all six shots directly into the middle of the stranger's forehead, just between his eyes.

"Are you through?" asked the stranger.

"Not yet," replied Surly, as he pulled out another revolver and shot another round into the stranger's forehead.

"Will that be all?" asked the stranger.

"Yes," said Surly, who turned on his heel, folded his arms, and sat down on a corner bench.

"Well then, check please!" called the stranger, rapping a coin against his glass. No one showed up. When they heard the shots, the whole staff hid in the attic.

So the stranger just left the change on the table, bid farewell to the detectives, and quietly went away.

Just then, Nosey Parker peered in through the first window, Alec Smart through the second, and Percy Witling through the third. Nosey leaped into the room first. "Where have you got him?" he inquired, then burst out laughing.

Alec Smart leaped in through the second window. "Foxelli seems to be rolling on the floor."

"Rolling seems to be somewhat surly," added Percy, jumping in through the third window. "And, you must admit that Surly doesn't look a bit bullish," he continued, adding insult to injury. "And I also believe that Bulloff isn't quite that foxy, after all."

Foxelli raised his head off the floor. "It's not as simple as it may possibly appear," he maintained. "That thief tied me up without moving a finger."

"He froze my hands in my pockets," growled Bulloff.

"And set the handcuffs on fire in my hands," whined Rolling.

"That's peanuts. I shot twelve bullets straight into his forehead and they didn't make a scratch," added Surly.

Nosey Parker, Alec Smart, and Percy Witling looked at each other.

"It seems to me," began Nosey Parker.

"—that the thief isn't a thief," continued Percy.

"—but really a magician," concluded Alec Smart.

"Come on and cheer up, men. He's done in," said Nosey Parker again. "We've brought a thousand soldiers with us—"

"—this inn is surrounded," continued Alec Smart.

"—and not a single mouse can squeeze through," added Percy Witling.

A thunderous shot sounded from a thousand rifles.

"He's finished," exclaimed the detectives.

The door flew open, and the Commander sprang into the room. "I dutifully report that my soldiers have surrounded the inn. I ordered that not a single mouse was to escape. But just then, a white dove with tender eyes fluttered out the doorway and circled around my head."

"Ah," they all cried, except Surly who said, "Well."

"With my saber I cut the little bird in half," the Commander went on, "and all one thousand soldiers fired a shot into it. The dove shattered into one thousand little pieces but each of those turned into a white butterfly and fluttered away, I report dutifully. Any further orders?"

Nosey Parker's eyes glistened. "Fine," he ordered. "Call in the army, the navy, and the marines. Send them all around the world, to every corner of the earth, to catch those butterflies." And so it was. And here let me tell you that those butterflies made an exceptionally lovely collection and all are displayed in the National History Museum to this day. When you are in Prague, you must go see it.

At the same time, Percy announced to the others, "You are of no use here, men. We'll manage fine without you."

Thus Foxelli, Rolling, Surly, and Bulloff went home dejected and empty-handed.

The three cousins conferred a long time about how to get the better of the magician. They smoked a heap of tobacco, they ate and drank all there was in the neighborhood but didn't come up with a thing. Finally, Alec Smart suggested, "Let's go outside and get some fresh air! We aren't getting anywhere this way!"

They had barely stepped outside when they saw the magician sitting in front of the door, watching them with interest and wondering what they would be up to next.

"Here he is," shouted Nosey Parker gaily, and with one bound, he grabbed the magician by the shoulder. But that very moment, the magician turned into a glittering snake, and Nosey, in a frenzy, let it drop to the ground.

Percy was there in a snap and threw his coat over the snake. But the snake became a tiny golden fly and slipped through a buttonhole into the air.

Alec Smart jumped up and scooped the golden fly into his cap, but the fly became a silvery brook that drifted away and pulled the cap down into its stream.

The three men dashed back to the tavern for beer mugs to catch the stream. But by then the stream had disappeared into the river Moldau. That is why to this day the Moldau, when it is in a good mood, looks like liquid silver; the river remembers the magician, hums, lost in thought, and glitters till one's head swims.

Nosey Parker, Alec Smart, and Percy Witling stood on the bank of the river Moldau and tried to figure out their next move. A silver fish bobbed out of the water and gazed at them with brilliant black eyes, the eyes of a magician, I'd say. So the three detectives bought themselves fishing rods and began to fish. To this day you can see them there as they sit in boats with their rods all day long, not saying a word. And they won't rest until they have caught that silvery, black-eyed fish.

Many other detectives tried to capture the magician, but all of their efforts were in vain. When they went after him speeding in a car, a doe suddenly would stick its head out from the underbrush and watch with black, tender, inquiring eyes. When they flew in an airplane, an eagle would pursue, fastening its proud, glowing eyes on them. And when they sailed on a ship, a dolphin would rise from the sea and fix its wise, quiet eyes on them. Even when they worked and brooded in their offices, flowers on their desks would at times glow and watch with curiosity and wonder; or their police dog would suddenly lift his head and observe them with eyes so human and beautiful as never before. The magician seemed to be watching them from everywhere, watching and then fading away. How in the world could they ever catch him?

How the Famous Sidney Hall Captured the Magician

Sidney Hall, the famous American detective, read about all this in the papers. He pondered the matter deeply and resolved to capture the magician by himself. He disguised himself as a millionaire, stuck a gun into his pocket, and left for Europe.

Soon after his arrival, he presented himself to the chief of police who, in turn, briefed him on all the details of the case. In closing, he said, "All things considered, it appears utterly impossible to bring the scoundrel to justice."

Sidney Hall smiled. "I'll bring him to you under arrest in forty days." "That's impossible!" cried the chief.

"Well, let's bet on a bowl of pears," suggested Sidney Hall. You see, Sidney Hall liked pears tremendously, and he enjoyed betting just as much. "It's a deal," agreed the chief. "And how, pray tell, will you go about it?"

"To start with, I must take a trip around the world. And to that end, I'll need quite a bit of cash."

So the police chief gave Sidney Hall a pile of money and, to appear smart, he said, "I bet I can read your mind. But this whole business must remain secret, for the magician must not find out we are after him."

"Oh no, on the contrary," said the detective. "As early as tomorrow, in all the papers of the world, you'll place a statement announcing that the famous Sidney Hall

has pledged to catch the magician within forty days. In the meantime, I have the honor of bidding you farewell."

Immediately afterward, Sidney Hall went to see a renowned traveler who had already made the journey around the world in fifty days, and he said, "Let's bet that I can make the journey around the world in forty days."

"That's impossible!" said the traveler. "Mr. Fox made the trip around the world in eighty days, I made it in fifty, but any faster is simply out of the question!"

"Well, shall we bet a thousand silver dollars?" suggested Sidney Hall.

And so they did.

The very same night Sidney Hall set off. A week later, a wire was received from Alexandria, Egypt: "On the track. Period. Signed, Sidney Hall."

Seven days later, another wire arrived, this time from Bombay, India: "The noose is tightening. All is well. Letter follows. Signed, Sidney Hall."

A little later, a letter arrived from Bombay, but it was written in a secret code that no one could decipher.

Eight days later, a homing pigeon flew in from Nagasaki, Japan, with a note fastened around its neck: "Zooming in. Expect me. Signed, Sidney Hall."

Then a dispatch arrived from San Francisco in America: "Caught cold. The rest OK. Buy pears. Signed, Sidney Hall."

The thirty-ninth day after he set out, a telegram finally came from Amsterdam, Holland: "Arriving tomorrow 7:15 P.M. Have the pears ready. Red Bartlett preferred. Sidney Hall."

The fortieth day, at 7:15 P.M. a train, its whistle blowing, rolled into the station. Out sprang Sidney Hall, followed by the magician, serious and pale, with downcast eyes. And awaiting them on the platform were all the detectives, astounded that the magician wasn't even hand-cuffed. Sidney Hall just beckoned to them. "See you to-night at the Blue Dog. But first, let me take this gentleman to jail." He hailed a taxicab and they both got in. Remembering something, Sidney Hall shouted from the cab, "And don't forget the pears!"

In the evening a bowl of gorgeous pears, surrounded by all the detectives, was awaiting Sidney Hall.

34

The detectives had begun to wonder if he would ever show up when a very old, haggard man selling boxes of matches opened the door and entered.

"We won't buy anything tonight, old man," the detectives told him.

"That's a pity," said the old man and began to shake and shiver all over, and hack, and cough, and choke. Breathless, he slumped into a chair.

"Mercy," screamed one of the detectives, "I hope he doesn't die on us."

"No need to worry," said the old man, chuckling and squirming. "I can't stand it any longer." It was then they realized that the old man was laughing so hard he couldn't stop. Tears rolled down his cheeks, his voice quivered, his face turned blue, and he groaned, "Children, children, I can't stand it any longer!"

"What are you up to, Grandpa?" inquired the detectives.

The old man got up, tottered to the table, selected the finest pear in the bowl, peeled it, and ate it at once. Then he tore off his false beard, false nose, false silver hair, and blue glasses, and revealed the smoothly shaven, smiling face of Sidney Hall.

"Listen guys," Sidney Hall said apologetically, "don't get upset with me. I've been suppressing laughter for the last forty days."

"When did you catch the magician?" asked the detectives in the same breath.

"Only yesterday," said the famous Sidney Hall. "But right from the very start I had to laugh at the prospect of duping him."

"Tell us, how in the world did you manage it?" the detectives insisted.

"Well, that's a long story," said Sidney Hall. "I'll tell you everything, but first, let me have another pear."

After eating the pear, he continued, "Listen, my friends. First and foremost, I must tell you that a good detective can't be an ass." Having said that, he looked around as if perhaps he expected to spot a donkey among those present.

"And what else?" asked the detectives.

"What else?" said Sidney Hall. "Next, a detective must be cunning. And third," he continued while peeling another pear, "he must be on the ball. Tell me, would you happen to know how to catch a mouse?"

"With a chunk of cheese," said the detectives.

"And how about a fish?"

"With a grub or an earthworm."

"And a magician?"

"No idea."

"A magician can be caught just like any other man," Sidney Hall lectured them, "through his own weakness, through the chink in his armor. First, you must find his foibles. And would you happen to know what the magician's weak spot was?"

"No idea."

"Curiosity," exclaimed Sidney Hall. "The magician had no shortcomings other than undying curiosity. He was unbelievably nosy. But now, I must have another pear."

After eating the pear, he continued. "You may have believed you were pursuing the magician, but in fact the magician was after you, following you, never losing sight of you. He was plagued with curiosity, and he needed to see all you would try against him. But he would meander when followed. I built my plan around his curiosity to orchestrate his downfall."

"What plan?" cried the detective eagerly.

"Well, listen, my friends. That trip around the world was only a ruse, it was a pleasure trip. I had always wanted to travel around the world, but somehow the opportunity had never presented itself—until the moment I arrived here. I knew then that the magician would always follow me to see how I'd catch him. He couldn't help it, as his curiosity propelled him. Very well, I said to myself, I'd have him with me around the world; I'd see a thing or two myself, and I wouldn't lose *him* from my sight. By that I mean he wouldn't lose sight of *me*. And to tickle his curiosity even more, I wagered to do it in forty days. But now, let me have this beautiful pear."

After eating it, he continued. "Nothing beats pears. So I took a gun and some money, disguised myself as a Swedish businessman, and took off. First to Genoa; that's in Italy, if you didn't know. On your way you see the beauty of the Alps. What a tremendous height! If a boulder breaks away from the top of a mountain, by the time it hits the bottom it's all covered with moss. From Genoa I wanted to go by boat to Alexandria, Egypt.

"Genoa is a lovely port, so beautiful in fact that every boat just runs there by itself. When the ships are a hundred miles away, they turn the motors off, the wheels stop turning, the sails are furled; the boats are so eager to get to the harbor they just sail of their own free will.

"My ship was to leave port at 4:00 P.M. sharp. At 3:50 I rushed to the harbor, but on the way I ran into a little girl in tears.

" 'Why are you crying, doll,' I asked.

" 'Boo-hoo,' the little darling cried. 'I got lost.'

" 'Well, if you got lost then you need to find yourself again.'

" 'But I've lost my mommy,' sobbed the tot, 'and I don't know where she is.'

" 'Now that's something else,' I said, taking the girl by the hand to look for her mother. I searched for an hour before I found her. But what then? It was 4:50. My ship must have been long gone. Because of that child, I'd lost a whole day. I walked toward the pier cheerless, but once there, I saw that the ship was still anchored. I stepped on board at once. 'You took your time, didn't you,' the captain said . 'You wouldn't have caught up with us if it hadn't been for the anchor getting caught somehow on the bottom. For an hour we couldn't get it up.' Needless to say, I was glad to hear that. But now, why don't I have another pear."

When he had eaten the pear, he went on. "This one was exceptionally delicious. So we sailed out into the Mediterranean. The blue of the sea is so beautiful that one doesn't know where the sky ends and the sea begins. Everywhere on the ship are signs to tell you where and what is up and where and what is down. Otherwise, you would get confused. 'Just the other day,' the captain told us, 'a boat got it all wrong and sailed off, not over the sea but across the sky, and since the sky is endless, the boat hasn't returned yet, and no one knows where it is.' So we sailed

over that sea till we reached Alexandria. Alexandria is a
great city because it was founded by Alexander the Great.

"From Alexandria I sent a telegram to give the
magician the impression that I was looking for him. In
truth I couldn't have cared less where he was. I sensed him
everywhere. When the seagulls and cormorants flew
around, or maybe an albatross with its flashing wings
sailed through the sky, I knew that one of them must have
been the magician following me. When a fish, emerging
from the deep sea, fixed its eyes on me, I felt as if the magician were watching through those eyes. And when the
swallows, on their flight across the sea, gathered on the
ship's riggings, I was almost certain that the white one,
the loveliest of them all, was *he*.

"From Alexandria, I sailed down the sacred river
Nile to Cairo. That city is so large it can't get a grasp of
itself. If it weren't for the very tall mosques and minarets
one sees from afar, the city would be lost, but looking at
those spires, even the farthest cottages know where they
are. And the weather is so hot that I took a bath in the
Nile. I left my clothes on the river bank and all I had on
was my swimming suit and my gun. Just then, an enormous crocodile crawled out of the river and devoured my
clothes and everything, including my watch and money. I
charged at him and fired six shots from the revolver. But
the bullets rebounded from his hide as if it were made of
steel. The crocodile looked at me and burst into roaring
laughter. And now, I'll have a pear."

After eating the pear, Sidney Hall continued,
"You know, gang, every crocodile can cry and holler like a
little kid. That's how he lures people into the water.

Thinking that a child is drowning, people hurry to the rescue, only to be ensnared and devoured by a crocodile. And this crocodile was so old and so wise that he had learned not only to cry like a baby but also to curse like a sailor, to sing like a opera star, and to talk like a man. It was rumored that he embraced the Turkish faith.

"To tell you the truth, I was quite uneasy. What was I to do with no clothes and no money? Suddenly, a dark-skinned Arab appeared and said to the monstrous beast, 'Tell me, croc, is it true that you have eaten this man's clothes and watch?'

" 'Correct,' said the crocodile.

" 'You nitwit,' said the Arab. 'That watch wasn't wound up. What good is a watch if it doesn't run?'

"The crocodile mused for a while, and then he addressed me. 'You, listen to me. I'll open my mouth a little, you'll reach into my stomach, take the watch out, wind it up, and put it back.'

" 'I wouldn't really mind,' I said, 'except you'd bite my hand off. Now how about if I stick this wooden pole upright in between your jaws first, just to make sure, you know, that you don't shut your dreadful muzzle on me.'

" 'I have no dreadful muzzle,' said the crocodile. 'But if you can't manage any other way, OK, put that stick in between my venerable jaws, but hurry up!'

"That's just what I did. I pulled from his stomach not only my watch but also my clothes, my shoes, and my hat as well, and I said to him: 'As a keepsake, I'll leave that stick with you, old fellow.' The crocodile tried to curse but he couldn't with his jaws wide open and braced with the stick. He tried to devour me, he tried to beg for mercy, but he couldn't. I took my time, got dressed, and said to him: 'In case you didn't know, let me tell you something. You've got an ugly, loathsome, stupid mug,' and I spat into it. Enraged, the crocodile burst into tears.

"I turned around, looking for the Arab who so cleverly had helped me out, but he was gone. And to this day, the crocodile swims in the Nile with his mouth wide open.

"From Alexandria, I sailed off to Bombay, disguised as an Indian raja. Boy, did I look grand! First, we sailed on the Red Sea. That sea is called red because it blushes shamefully for being so small. You see, when all the seas were young and tiny and had not yet finished growing, the Red Sea played on the shore with the Arab children. Time passed by so fast that the sea forgot to grow, although God Almighty had provided lovely sand in all the surrounding deserts, just so the sea could make a soft bed for itself. Then, at the very last moment, the sea remembered it had to grow, but by then it was too late, and the sea grew only in length. Even then a strip of land remained between the sea and the Mediterranean with which it was supposed to be united. The Red Sea was plagued so much by its size that people took pity and linked both seas with a canal. And from then on, it hasn't blushed quite as much.

"One night, after we had sailed past the Red Sea, while I slept in my cabin, someone knocked on my door. I went to open it, but no one was there. Then I heard two sailors approaching my cabin. 'We'll kill him,' whispered one of them, 'and take all those pearls and diamonds.' Upon my soul, friends, all the pearls and diamonds I wore were made of glass. 'Wait here,' whispered the other, 'I forgot the knife upstairs.' When he left, I grabbed the first by his throat, gagged him, dressed him as the raja, and laid him on my berth, all tied up. Then I put on his clothes and went outside to take his position. When his pal returned with the knife, I told him, 'Don't bother to kill the raja, I've strangled him already. But while I keep watch, why don't you go in and take his pearls and diamonds.' The moment he entered my cabin, I locked him in and went to the captain. 'Captain,' I said, 'I've received some strange visitors: come see for yourself.' When the captain saw what had happened, he had both sailors flogged. I gathered the rest of the crew, showed them my pearls and diamonds, and said, 'Just look how much these pearls and diamonds matter to a wise man!' and with that, I tossed all my glass jewels overboard. Everyone began to bow to me and call, 'Oh, wise is the raja, and sublime!'—But who was the man who had knocked on my door and saved my life? That I never found out. And now, I'll eat this lovely, large pear."

Sidney Hall hadn't even finished when he began to speak with his mouth full. "With good luck on our side, we reached Bombay. India, my friends, is a large and strange country. It's so hot that even water is completely dry and needs to be watered so as not to evaporate. The forests are so thick, there's no room for trees, so they're called rain forests. After a rain, everything grows tremendously, entire temples spring from the ground, just like mushrooms. That's why so many temples are in Benares. And there are as many monkeys as sparrows, and those monkeys are so tame they'll climb right into your bedroom. When you wake in the morning, it's not inconceivable that you may find a monkey in your bed instead of yourself. That's how tame those beasts are. And the snakes are so long that when they look at their own tails they can't even recognize them. A snake like that, believing a bigger snake is chasing it, slithers away and dies in misery chasing itself to death. And I haven't yet mentioned elephants who are at home in India. All things considered, India is a large country.

"From Bombay I again sent a wire and a coded letter, just to make the magician believe I had some ingenious plan up my sleeve."

"What was in that letter?" asked the detectives.

"I've deciphered half of it," one of the detectives bragged hastily.

"Then no doubt you're smarter than I," said the famous Sidney Hall, "for I wouldn't be able to decipher it myself. I just scribbled some mumbo jumbo to make it look like a coded message. From Bombay I went by train to Calcutta. Indian trains have bathtubs instead of seats so the passengers can cool off a little. The train made its way through deserts and rain forests. On the way, I saw the dreadful eyes of a tiger gleaming in the bush, and on the fords over the river the wise gaze of a white elephant's lordly eyes. A bold mountain eagle raced with our train, and a rainbow-colored butterfly fluttered by the window. Everywhere, I could sense the presence of the magician.

"Not far from Calcutta we came close to the holy river Ganges. That river is so wide that if you throw a stone across to the other side it will take an hour and a half to land. As we traveled alongside the holy river, I saw a

woman washing her laundry. She either must have bent
over too far or something else must have happened for just
as we passed by, she fell in and began to drown. I leaped
from the fast-moving train and dragged that clumsy Indian
out of the river. I'm convinced that each and every one of
you fellows would have done the same."

The detectives murmured in agreement.

"I shouldn't mislead you, though," continued
Sidney Hall. "This time I didn't come off so easily. As I
was struggling to tug that woman out of the water, a
deadly crocodile attacked me and severely bit my hand. I
managed to get the woman to the shore, but then I collapsed and blacked out. For four days, old Indian women
nursed me, and, well, I received this ring from them as a
keepsake. To make the story short, let me just tell you that
people, wherever they live, know how to express gratitude. And whether dark pagans or naked men in the jun-
gles of India, they aren't a bit less kind than any of us, and
that's the truth.

"All the same I lost five days and this nearly cost
me my bet. Sitting on the bank of the holy river I thought,
now I'll never make it in forty days. There go a thousand
silver dollars to the devil, and a bowl of pears as well. And
as I was thinking, a silly little boat flying sails made of
mats which the natives call a dinghy, came sailing by.
From the keel, three brown Malayan oafs were grinning at
me, showing their teeth, as if about to eat me up. 'Nia
namia pche chem Nagasaki,' one of them blubbered. 'Listen, you clown,' I told him, 'do you think I understand
you?' 'Nia namia pche chem Nagasaki,' he jabbered again,
in a manner he probably thought was cute. 'Nagasaki' I

understood. That's a port in Japan, and that's where I wanted to sail next. 'To Nagasaki in this bucket? Not on your life!' 'Nia,' he tells me and jabbers some more, pointing to his dinghy, then to the sky, and then to his heart. In short, he was trying to tell me I should go with him. 'Not for a bowl of pears,' I was about to tell him when those three devils jumped on me, knocked me to the ground, wrapped me in the mats, and dumped me like a sack of potatoes into their dinghy. While all this was happening my thoughts weren't of the kindest sort, to say the least, but they were interrupted when, eventually, I fell asleep. I awoke not in the dinghy, but ashore. An enormous chrysanthemum had replaced the sun above me. All around, the trees were beautifully lacquered, each grain of sand on the shore was carefully washed and polished, and the neatness of the place suggested that I was in Japan. And when I met the first pigtailed man with slanted eyes, I asked him: 'Would you tell me where I am?' 'Nagasaki,' he replied, smiling.

"Listen, guys. I'm not known to be half-witted," Sidney Hall continued pensively. "But to comprehend how on that miserable dinghy I had made the journey from Calcutta to Nagasaki in one night when it takes the fastest ocean liner ten days . . . that was beyond my comprehension. And now, I'll eat this pear."

After he had peeled it carefully and eaten it, he went on.

"Japan is a large and unusual country and her people are cheerful and bright. They know how to make china teacups so thin that they don't even need any china to make them. They hold up their thumbs, spin them in the air, put a layer of paint on top, and the cup is finished. And if I told you how the Japanese can paint, you wouldn't believe me. I saw a painter whose brush fell out of his hand on a blank sheet of paper, and as it rolled down, it painted a whole landscape, with cottages and trees, with people in the streets, wild geese in the sky, and all. When I marveled at it, the painter said to me: 'This pales in comparison with what my master could do. Once in the rain, he soiled his venerable slippers. When the mud had dried a little, he showed them to us: one slipper was painted with a scene of dogs and hunters, scouting for rabbits, and the other had a painting of children playing school.'

"From Nagasaki I sailed to San Francisco in America. During that trip nothing remarkable happened except that our ocean liner got wrecked and began to sink. Quickly, we all jumped into the lifeboats. When they were all filled, two sailors shouted from the sinking ship: 'There's one more lady here! Can she squeeze in?' Some people yelled: 'No!' but I hollered: 'Sure, she can! Let her come over!' So to make room for her, they threw me overboard. I didn't even protest too much. Ladies first, always, I thought. After the ship sank, and the lifeboats disappeared in the distance, I was left all alone and forsaken on the high seas. I sat on a plank and rocked on the waves—which would have been quite pleasant if it hadn't been so wet. I floated for a day and a night and when I had just begun to fear that it would all come to a bad end, a tin box with rockets in it came floating along.

"What was I to do with rockets? I thought at first. I would have preferred some pears instead. Then I got the hint. When the blackest night fell, I fired the first rocket. It flew very high and shone like a meteor; the second was like a star, and the third like a sun; the fourth sang, and the fifth shot so high it got stuck right among the stars and there it shines to this day. I was having quite a good time when a large ship came up and took me on board. 'Dear fellow, had it not been for those rockets, you would have drowned,' the captain said. 'As soon as we saw those rockets gleaming ten miles in the distance, we suspected that someone was calling for help.' And in honor of that good captain, I'll have this pear."

After eating it, he continued cheerfully. "I stepped onto American soil in San Francisco. America, my dear friends, is my homeland, and—what is there to say— America is America. It makes no sense to tell you about America, for you would never believe anything I told you. Such an unusual and vast country it is. Well, let me just tell you that I got on the Great Union Pacific Railroad and took off for New York. In New York, the buildings are so tall they can't even be finished. The masons and the roofers spend all morning climbing the ladder and once they reach the top and have their lunch up in the air, it's time to climb down for bed. So it goes, day after day. All in all, nothing can beat America. And let me tell you, a person who doesn't like his homeland as much as I love America is an old fool.

"I left the States on an ocean liner heading for Amsterdam, Holland. On the way—on the way—well, the nicest and the happiest thing happened to me on the way from America to Holland. By golly, it must have been the best joke of my entire expedition."

"What happened?" the detectives cried eagerly.

"Well," said Sidney Hall, blushing, "I got engaged. On the ship I met a girl, quite lovely, I'd say. Her name is Alice, and no one in the whole world, including you, is lovelier—definitely not," added Sidney Hall, after a long deliberation. "But do you think I told her how much I liked her? The last day of the passage came and went, and still I had not told her anything. And now, let me have this pear."

After he had properly enjoyed it, Sidney Hall continued. "The last evening, as I was walking on deck, Miss Alice approached me on her own. 'Mr. Hall,' she said, 'have you by any chance ever been to Genoa?' 'Yes, miss, I have.' 'And didn't you see there a little girl who got lost?' asked Alice. 'Well, yes, ma'am, I did. An old fool gave her a hand.'

"Alice fell silent and then went on. 'And weren't you also in India?' 'I was.' 'And didn't you see a young man who bravely jumped from a running train into the river Ganges to save a drowning washerwoman?' 'Yes, I did,' I answered, somewhat embarrassed. 'He too must have been an old fool, miss. No one in his right mind would have done anything that foolish.'

"Alice remained silent for a while, looking at me in an odd, sweet way.

" 'Is it true, Mr. Hall,' I heard her saying again, 'is it true that a noble man sacrificed himself at sea, letting a lady have his place on a lifeboat?' I began to feel hot all over. 'Well, miss, if I am not altogether mistaken, yes, an old scarecrow did take a swim that way the other day.'

"Alice placed both her hands into mine, blushed, and said, 'Do you realize, Mr. Hall, what an awfully nice person you are? Don't you think that for what you did for that little girl in Genoa, and for the Indian washerwoman, and for the unknown lady—don't you think that for all that, everybody must love you?'

"At that point, dear God himself must have pushed me into taking Alice in my arms. Thus we became engaged. Then I asked her, 'Listen, Alice, who told you all those silly things about me? As God is above me, I never bragged to anyone about any of them.'

" 'Well, tonight, as I was looking out to sea and thinking of you, a little, tiny black woman came to me, and told me all that.' Wanting to thank the little black lady, we went searching for her, but couldn't find her. Now you know how I got engaged on that ship," concluded Sidney Hall, wiping his gleaming eyes.

"And what about the magician?" called out the detectives.

"What about him?" retorted the famous Sidney Hall. "He fell victim to his own curiosity just as I had foreseen. When I stayed overnight in Amsterdam, somebody knocked on my door. In walked the magician himself. He looked pale and troubled. 'Mr. Hall,' he addressed me, 'I can't bear it any longer. Would you tell me how you want to catch me?'

" 'Dear Mr. Magician,' I replied gravely. 'That I won't tell you, for if I told you, I'd give away my plans and you'd flee!'

" 'Ah,' lamented the magician, 'have pity on me! I can't sleep for curiosity.'

" 'All right then,' I told him. 'But first you must swear that from now on you're my prisoner and that you won't attempt to escape.'

" 'I swear,' cried the magician.

" 'My plan has worked,' I said, getting up. 'I had bet solely on your curiosity. I knew you were following me on dry land and on the sea to discover what I was up to. I knew that in the end you'd come to me, just as you've done now. I knew further that you'd give up your freedom merely to satisfy your curiosity. And now, my prediction has been fulfilled.'

"Turning pale and glum, the magician said, 'You, Mr. Hall, are a great trickster, outwitting even a magician.'

"And that's the whole story, boys."

All the detectives burst into tremendous laughter and congratulated the happy American on his success. Sidney Hall smiled with satisfaction and poked around in the bowl for a nice pear. He pounced on one wrapped in paper. He opened the wrapper and found a message:

"A souvenir to Mr. Hall from the Genovese tot."

Sidney Hall reached into the bowl, found another pear wrapped in paper, undid it, and read:

"The washerwoman from the bank of the Ganges River wishes Mr. Hall a good appetite."

He unwrapped another pear and read:

"To my noble rescuer with thanks—the grateful woman from the sinking ship."

Sidney Hall reached into the bowl a fourth time, unwrapped a fourth pear, and read:

"Thinking of you. Alice."

The last pear in the bowl was the most beautiful. Sidney Hall sliced it, and found a folded letter inside. The envelope read: To Mr. Sidney Hall. Briskly, he opened the letter and read:

"A man who has a secret should beware of fever. The wounded detective in his feverish sleep on the bank of the Ganges babbled out his secret plan. It was a plan of a long-eared donkey. Your friend did not want to deprive you of the reward which was put on his head; hence he let himself be voluntarily incarcerated. The reward you'll get is his wedding present to you."

Sidney Hall's astonishment was boundless. "Finally," he uttered, "it all fits together. Am I really an old fool? It was the magician himself who held the anchor in the ground while I was running all around Genoa with that little girl. It was the magician who, disguised as an Arab, helped me get away from that crocodile. It was the magician who woke me when the two sailors were about to kill me. The magician overheard my plan while I was delirious, after my accident in the river Ganges. The magician sent the mysterious dinghy to take me to Nagasaki without delay. The magician handed out the box of rockets that saved my life at sea. The magician transformed himself into a little black lady and helped me win Alice's heart. And finally, the magician deliberately pretended to be dumb and curious and helped me win the reward set on his head. I wanted to outsmart him but he is much smarter than I and besides, he's more generous. There isn't anyone like the magician! Together, men: Long live the magician!"

"Hail to the magician!" the detectives yelled so loud that all the windowpanes in the city cracked.

The Magician Behind Bars

Soon after the famous Sidney Hall had arrested the magician, judicial proceedings were begun to recover the stolen cat.

The judge, Doctor Corpus Juris, as fat as he was stern, sat enthroned behind a large desk. And on the defendant's bench sat the magician, handcuffed.

"Rise, villain," roared Doctor Corpus. "You are accused of stealing Youra, the royal cat, born in this country, age one year. Do you plead guilty, scamp?"

"Yes, I do," said the magician softly.

"You lie, scoundrel," thundered the judge. "I don't believe one word you say. Prove it! Hey you, call the witness. Our most serene Highness, the princess."

They brought in the princess to testify.

"My darling little princess," Corpus twittered sweetly. "Tell me, my dear, did this wretched man steal Youra, your noble cat?"

"Yes, he did," said the princess.

"You see, you skunk," roared the judge at the magician, "you were proven guilty! Say, how did you do it?"

"Well, I did it . . . " began the magician, "well, she fell on my head."

"Hogwash! You wretched liar!" bellowed the judge and turned to the princess whom he addressed in his softest voice. "My darling little princess, how did this scoundrel steal your most venerable cat?"

"Just as he said he did," said the princess.

"You see, you fibber, you," shrieked the judge. "Now we know how you stole her! And why did you steal her, you rogue?"

"Because when she fell, she broke her leg. I took her under my coat to set her leg right and to bandage it."

"Every word you say is a big lie!" Doctor Corpus cried. "Call in the next witness, the proprietor of the tavern in Strašnice."

So they brought in the owner of the tavern.

"Know anything about this criminal?" yelled the judge.

"All I know, Your Honor," said the man timidly, "is that the accused entered my tavern, removed a black cat from under his coat, and bound her leg."

"Hm," muttered Doctor Corpus. "You too could be lying. And then what did he do with that revered little pet?"

"Then, well," the innkeeper said, "then he let her go, and the cat ran away."

"Aha! Tormentor of animals!" hollered the judge, pouncing on the magician. "You let her go and she ran away! Where is the king's cat now?"

"She just might have run back to the place where she was born," said the magician. "Cats do that, you know."

"Ha, you insolent miscreant!" roared the judge. "You want to lecture me? Dear princess," he again addressed the princess in the softest voice, "how much does Your Highness think the highly esteemed Youra is worth?"

"Not for half of the kingdom would I give her away," the princess declared.

"You see, you good-for-nothing," the judge roared, "you have stolen half the kingdom. Such a crime is punishable by the death sentence, you villain!"

Upon hearing that, the princess's heart filled with pity for the magician. "Maybe," she said hastily, "just maybe I'd trade Youra for a slice of cake."

"And what, Your Highness, would a slice of cake be worth?"

"Well, a slice of hazelnut torte is a nickel, strawberry costs a dime, and whipped cream adds an extra nickel."

"And which cake would Your Highness trade for Youra?"

"Strawberry with whipped cream, I guess."

"Huh, cutthroat!" yelled the judge at the magician. "That's the same as stealing three nickels. Three days in jail are coming to you, according to the law. Now, off to the slammer with you, you archvillain, you infamous thief, you marauder, you! Your Highness," he gently addressed the princess once again, "I have the honor to thank you for your wise and most thoughtful testimony. Please relate to His Majesty, your dear father, the loyal respects from his most obedient, most faithful and most upright judge, Doctor Corpus."

They threw the magician in jail and gave him a slice of stale bread with some putrid water in a mug. But he just sat and smiled, and his eyes started glowing brighter and shinier. At midnight, he rose and waved his hand. Sweet music sounded and the air became fragrant

with the scent of thousands of flowers. Indeed, in the barren prison yard bushes of blooming roses sprang forth, tufts of lilies raised their chalices toward the white moon, flower beds of pansies and lilies-of-the-valley blossomed, iris and peony swayed with heavy flowers, white and red hawthorn swelled, and on a branch, a nightingale broke into song.

A condemned murderer awoke in his cell; an arsonist, on his hard bed, rubbed the sleep out of his eyes; a thug serving his sentence arose bewildered; a thief cried out in awe; and a swindler, repenting for his sins, folded his hands in prayer, unable to understand what was happening. For the cold, dank prison walls opened and arched into a lovely colonnade. The prisoners' dirty beds were sheathed in white linen; bolts and bars vanished, and a few stone steps led straight to the flowering garden.

"Francis," the murderer growled at the arsonist, "are you asleep?"

"No, man, but I must be dreaming. It sure looks like I'm not in the can any more."

"Guys," the thug cried, "I must have died and gone to heaven!"

"Heaven!" exclaimed the swindler. "Is there any heaven left for me? I too had a beautiful dream, as if I were in Paradise."

"That's no dream," the thief said. "This is for real, you can touch all of it. Right now I am touching a lily. Ah, if only I could have it!"

"You may," said a firm and pleasant voice. Amid the prisoners, in a white robe, stood the magician. "The lily is yours, my friend!"

"Sir, are you a warden here?" asked the arsonist bashfully.

"No, friends, I am a convict just like you," the magician replied. "Sentenced and all. Now, this garden is ours. The tables under the trees are laid for us. The nightingale sings for us. For us the roses bloom. Come friends, dinner is served!"

They all sat down at a bountiful table and began to feast. The magician served them rare delicacies and wine. As he poured wine for the swindler, the man cast down his eyes and said softly, "No, please, not for me!"

"Won't you have some wine?" asked the magician.

"No, I don't deserve it, sir. I have caused the downfall of too many people. How can I enjoy wine now?"

The magician's eyes lit up, but he said nothing as he served the rest. While filling the murderer's glass his hand quivered, and a few drops of red wine spilled on the tablecloth.

"Sir," the murderer exclaimed in desperation, "why does that wine remind me of blood? Why have I spilled innocent blood? Woe on me, wretched man that I am!"

The magician said nothing, but his eyes lit up even more. When he offered wine to the thug, the criminal exclaimed, "How could I drink wine! I struck people to death out of greed, and I willfully lamed them; I struck the hand that offered me friendship; I tormented those who loved me most!"

The magician's face was all aglow now, but he didn't utter a word. He turned toward the thief, and offered the most beautiful fruit. "Take some, my friend," he said sincerely, "it's all yours."

"Sir," cried the thief, "I took what wasn't mine; don't allow me now to take what perhaps I might receive."

The magician smiled brightly and approached the arsonist. "Help yourself to some fruit," he said. "It will refresh you."

"Dear sir," the arsonist objected, "I set fire to the roof above the heads of those who were kind to me. Now they're paupers and have to beg for a slice of bread. If only I could refresh those I have harmed!"

Now the magician's eyes beamed like stars. He stood erect and said, "For years you've been famished and thirsty; for years you've not tasted sweetness with your tongues or felt joy in your hearts. So why won't you eat and drink now, feast and enjoy? Help yourself to everything, it's all yours!"

At that moment, the sound of many steps was heard in the garden. A crowd of paupers, lame people, and beggars approached the feast.

"My God!" cried the swindler. "Here come the people I made poor."

"I see the man I killed!" screamed the assassin, partly in panic, partly in joy.

"Good Lord," the thug exclaimed, "these are the lame and wounded people I injured!"

"And here are those I robbed!" the thief burst out.

"Woe is me!" moaned the arsonist. "I set fire to the roof over these poor people's heads!"

The swindler sprang up and carried food and wine to those he had reduced to poverty; the murderer tore the tablecloth in shreds, knelt down beside the man he had murdered, and with his tears washed the man's wounds and bound them up; the thug poured wine and oil on the wounds of those he had hurt; the thief removed the gold and silver flatware from the table and urged those he had robbed to take it; and the arsonist, seeing it all, said tearfully, "Woe is me, what can I give you, poor beggars, whom I deprived of everything?" Then he picked all the flowers from the garden and showered them on the paupers.

The swindler fed those he had made poor; the assassin bound the wounds of his murdered victims; the thug nursed the wounded; the thief offered presents to those he had robbed; and the arsonist covered the beggars' rags with flowers. Keeping nothing for themselves, they ushered their guests to the palace and soothed them to sleep on white linen beds while they lay down on the floor.

Alone, the magician remained in the garden, his arms folded, his eyes shining like two stars. A sweet, gentle sleep descended on the jail.

With a bang, the jailer walked in.

"Get up, you scoundrels," he roared. "You've been asleep for three days."

The convicts arose instantly and realized they were lying on the floor beside their hard, soiled beds; the airy columns had turned back into damp prison walls, and the forlorn yard was bare, with no trace of flowers or blooming trees. All that was left were a few rose petals and lily leaves strewn on the ground.

"Did you say we've been asleep for three days?" wondered the murderer.

"What? Was it only a dream?" cried the arsonist.

"Warden, wasn't anyone here besides us?" asked the thief.

"There was," the warden growled. "The one who stole the king's cat stood stock-still in his cell for three days, his eyes shining like two stars. And this morning, after he had served his time, he was gone. A naughty rascal, that one! Before he vanished into thin air, he cast a spell on our honorable judge, Doctor Corpus. His Honor sprouted donkey's ears. Well, keep moving, you scoundrels, up, get up!"

The treadmill was back in motion, but something had changed. Now, the stinking water in their mugs tasted like the sweetest wine, the stale bread like delicious cake, the jail breathed out a lovely fragrance of flowers, and at night, when the convicts went to sleep, their beds were covered with the purest white linen. Every night since, a restful peace, free from remorse and suffering, has reigned over the jail.

The End of the Fairy Tale

When the princess heard in the courtroom that Youra, her cat, might have run back to the place where she was born, she immediately dispatched a courier to the granny's cottage.

Speeding on his horse, flying until sparks shot up from beneath the hooves, the courier came upon Vašek, the old woman's grandson, holding a black cat in his arms in front of his grandma's cottage.

"Vašek," the courier cried, "the princess wants her Youra back."

Vašek's heart throbbed at the thought of losing Youra, but he said, "I'll bring her to the princess myself."

With Youra in a pouch, Vašek hurried to the palace and headed straight to the princess.

"Here, Your Highness, is our cat," he said. "If it's Youra, you may keep her."

Vašek opened the bag, but Youra did not leap forward as daringly as she had the first time from granny's basket. She limped on one leg, poor thing.

"I'm not sure if this is our Youra," said the princess, in doubt. "Our Youra didn't limp, not even a tiny bit. I'll tell you what, let's call Buffino."

When Buffino saw Youra, he began to wag his tail till it wiggled, but what he said to her, and what she answered, none of them understood.

"It's our Youra all right," cried the princess. "Buffino recognized her. Now what shall I give you for bringing her back? Money maybe?"

Vašek blushed and said quickly, "I don't want any money, Your Highness. Grandma has so much she doesn't know what to do with it."

"Well, then, how about a slice of cake?" asked the princess.

"Oh no, thanks. We've got as many cakes as we like," said Vašek.

"Well, would you like one of my toys maybe?" mused the princess.

"No, thanks," Vašek waved his hand. "With my jackknife I can carve out any toy I want."

Now the princess really had no idea what to offer.

"Then why don't you tell me what you'd like," she finally suggested.

"Well, Your Highness," stuttered Vašek, turning crimson as a poppy.

"Please, Vašek, please tell me," the princess insisted.

"I dare not tell you," protested Vašek with his face now crimson up to his ears.

In turn, the princess blushed like a peony. "And why," she said, "won't you tell me?"

"Because," poor Vašek said, "you wouldn't give it to me anyway."

The princess blushed like a rose. "And what," she said haltingly, "if I gave it to you?"

Vašek shook his head, "You won't."

"But what if I will?"

"You mustn't," said Vašek sadly. "I'm not a prince."

"Look over there, Vašek," the princess said quickly, and when Vašek turned away, she hastily gave him a kiss on his cheek. Before he could get over his surprise, the princess hid in the corner with Youra in her arms, her face buried in Youra's fur.

Vašek was flushed and his face glowed. "I have to leave now," he said. "God bless you, Your Highness."

"Vašek," whispered the princess, "was that what you wanted?"

"It was, Your Highness," Vašek blurted out ardently. Just then, the ladies-in-waiting walked into the room, and Vašek made a hasty departure.

Cheerfully, he trotted home. He stopped in the woods only long enough to carve a nice little boat from the bark of a tree, and with the little boat in his pocket, he scampered home.

When he drew near, he saw Youra sitting on the doorstep, cleaning her fur with her injured leg.

"Grandma," Vašek hollered, "I just took Youra to the castle!"

"Well, my boy," said his granny, "it's a cat's nature to always return to the place she was born, even if it's miles and miles away. Try to take her back again in the morning."

In the morning, Vašek scurried back to the palace with Youra. "Your Highness," he panted, "here, I've brought Youra back again. She ran away from you, the little imp, straight back to our cottage."

"My, you do run fast! Like the wind!" said the princess.

"Do you think you might like this little boat, Your Highness?" Vašek prattled.

"Let me have it," said the princess. "And what shall I give you for Youra today?"

"I don't know," replied Vašek, and immediately flushed to the roots of his hair.

"Just tell me," whispered the princess, and blushed even more.

"I won't."

"Tell me!"

"I won't."

The princess bowed her head and poked the toy boat with her finger. "Would you perhaps," she said at last, "would you want the same as yesterday?"

"Maybe," Vašek blurted out. And when he had received the kiss, he ran home, filled with delight.

At the willows, he tarried a while and whittled a lovely, sweet-sounding whistle.

When he got home, Youra was sitting on the doorstep, patting her whiskers with her paw. "Grandma," Vašek called out again, "Youra's back!"

"Well then, tomorrow you'll pick her up and take her back to the palace. She may get used to the place yet."

In the morning, Vašek put Youra in a sack, slung it on his back, and ran back to the palace.

"Your Highness," he exclaimed, "Princess, Youra ran back to us again."

But the Princess looked sullen and said nothing.

"Look, princess, I carved this whistle yesterday," Vašek boasted.

"Fine, let me have it," said the princess, out of sorts. Vašek shuffled his feet and wondered why the princess was so grumpy.

The princess blew the whistle, and upon hearing its lovely sound, she said, "I know you're doing this on purpose. With Youra, I mean. So that I, so that you, so that you'll get your reward—the same as yesterday."

Vašek was pained; he snapped his cap on, and said, "If that's what you believe, so be it. I will never come back again."

Crestfallen, Vašek dragged himself home. As he drew near he saw Youra, sitting on the doorstep, licking herself after a hearty gulp of milk. Vašek sat down beside her, took her in his lap, and remained still.

Suddenly, in a flurry, the king's courier rode up on his horse.

"Vašek," he yelled, "His Majesty bids you to bring Youra to the palace!"

"It's no use. A cat will always return to her birthplace."

"Never mind," said the courier, "the princess doesn't seem to care. She said she wouldn't mind if you brought Youra back every day."

Vašek shook his head. "I told the princess I wouldn't come."

Just then Grandmother came out on the porch. "Sir, remember, a dog clings to his master, a cat to her cottage. Youra will always stick to this cottage."

The courier whirled and galloped off at full speed to the palace. The next day, an enormous wagon drawn by one hundred horses pulled up in front of Granny's cottage.

The horseman climbed down from his saddle and called out, "Grandma, His Majesty says that if a cat clings to her cottage, I must bring back the cottage with the cat, and you and Vašek as well. His Majesty seems to believe that the cottage will fit quite well into the royal gardens."

Many people gathered and helped load the whole cottage onto the wagon. The horseman cracked his whip, and with a "Giddy-up!" one hundred horses pulled, and the wagon with the cottage sallied forth and rolled toward the palace. On the wagon, in the doorway to the cottage, sat Granny, Vašek, and Youra. That's when the old woman recalled the Queen Mother's dream about a black cat who was to bring the future king to the palace. She also remembered the Queen Mother's dream about the future king who would arrive with his entire house. She mused but said nothing.

In the palace, the wagon was greeted with great merriment. The cottage was unloaded in the garden, and it never occurred to Youra to run away again. She lived there with Granny and Vašek, just as she always had. When the princess wanted to play with Youra, she had only to go to the cottage and get her. And since, by all accounts, the princess liked Youra a great deal, she was at the cottage every day and became fast friends with Vašek.

What followed thereafter does not belong to our story. If Vašek really did become king in that country when he grew up, it was not because of the cat, nor was it by virtue of his friendship with the princess. It was because of the mighty and heroic deeds that the princely Vašek carried out for the good of his whole country.

The
Dog's
Tale

B ack in the days when my grandfather's wagon used to make the rounds of the villages in our parish, bringing bread to the villagers, and then returning to the mill with a wagonful of golden grain, everybody knew Peanut. Peanut, they would have told you, was the little dog that sat on the coach box beside old Šulitka the horseman and looked as if he were in charge of the whole business. And when the wagon slowed down, struggling up the hillside, Peanut started to bark, the wheels began to churn faster, old Šulitka cracked his whip, Ferda and Žanka, my grandpa's two horses, quickened their gallop, and the wagon clattered into the village in all its splendor, strewing the beautiful scent of God's bounty. Well, children, that's how the late Peanut used to ride around the whole parish.

Oh yes, in Peanut's time there were none of those cranky, crazy cars zooming everywhere. In those days one drove slowly, with class, and with a clamor. Nowadays, no driver can crack his whip or click his tongue at the horses the way the late Šulitka did—God rest his soul—and no driver has a companion as intelligent as Peanut, pushing forward, barking, and spreading terror. Today, when a car flies by it leaves behind its stench and if you look where it's gone, you can't even see it through the dust! Believe me, Peanut was a far more competent driver. A half hour before he pulled in, people pricked up their ears, sniffed, and said, "Aha!" Knowing that their bread was on the way, they would come out and stand on their doorsteps to welcome him with, "Good morning!" Then, Grandfather's wagon would roll into the village, with Šulitka clicking his tongue, and Peanut barking on the driver's seat. Hop! he would leap on Žanka's rump (did she have a rump!—God bless her!—wide as a table that could seat four people), and dance on Žanka's back, running from her collar to her tail and back to her collar again, barking with joy. "Ruff, ruff, what a drive! Žanka, Ferda and I, hurray!" Everyone marveled, "Good Lord, our daily bread's arriving, and with such pomp and glory as if the emperor himself were coming!" Well, as I said, drivers like those in Peanut's day I haven't seen since!

Did Peanut know how to bark! It sounded as if he were shooting off a gun. Bang!—to the right, at the geese who would run off in fright, not stopping till they found themselves at the market in Poličky, completely perplexed at how they had gotten there. Bang!—to the left, with such vigor that all the village pigeons flew up, circled and landed somewhere around Žaltman, close to the Prussian side of the border. That's how heartily Peanut could bark, that silly cur. It was a miracle his tail didn't fly off, as he wagged so lustily and with such joy over his mischief. Granted, he had something to be proud of. No general, mind you, not even a congressman, had that powerful a voice!

Yet, there was a time when Peanut did not know how to bark at all, although he was already quite grown, with teeth that tore up Grandpa's Sunday boots. Besides, I think I should tell you how Grandpa found Peanut (or it may have happened the other way around). Once, late at night, when Grandpa was coming home from the pub in a happy mood, singing along, perhaps to keep the evil spirits at bay, it so happened that he lost the tune and had to stop to look for it. While he was searching, he heard a whimper, a squeak, and a squeal coming from somewhere at his feet. He crossed himself and groped around to find out what it was. He felt a warm, shaggy, velvety soft little ball, that fit into the palm of his hand. As soon as he picked it up, it stopped whimpering and began sucking his finger as if it were made of honey. "I must have a look at it, whatever it is," Grandpa thought, and carried it home to the mill. Poor Grandma had been waiting for Grandpa to bid him good night, but now, even before she could bawl him out, Grandpa, the sly fellow, said, "Helen, see what I've brought you." Grandma held the furball up to the candle-light and, by golly, it was a puppy, a puny pup still blind and tawny, like a fresh hazelnut cracked out of its shell. "Now look at that. A puppy," said Grandpa. "Tell me, my dear, to whom do you belong?" Grandpa asked. Naturally, the little pup said nothing. He quivered on the table like a bundle of misery until his tail began to twitch, whimpering sorrowfully. Then, my goodness, a tiny puddle appeared beneath him, growing larger all the time, like a bad conscience. "Karl, Karl," said Grandma sternly, shaking her head. "Have you lost your mind? Without his mother, this puppy will wither away." Grandpa became frightened. "All right, Helen, now move quickly," he said, "warm some milk and get me a dinner roll." Grandma got everything ready, and Grandpa dipped a soft crumb into the milk, wrapped it up in the corner of his hanky, and made such a wonderful nipple that the puppy sucked it until his tummy looked like a drum.

"Karl, Karl," said Grandma, shaking her head again, "are you out of your mind? Tell me who'll warm the pup so he won't die of cold?" But Grandfather wasn't

about to be deterred. He took the puppy and carried him straight to the stable. Good gracious, was it hot in there from all the hot air that Ferda and Žanka puffed out! Both horses had been asleep, but when their master walked in they lifted their heads and followed him with their wise, gentle eyes. "Listen, Žanka, listen, Ferda," said Grandpa, "this is Peanut. Here, take care of him, and don't harm him!" Then, he placed little Peanut on the straw in front of the horses. Žanka sniffed the odd tiny creature and, smelling the scent of her master's hands, she whispered to Ferda, "He's all right." And so it was.

Peanut stayed in the stable. He was fed through the nipple made out of a handkerchief until his eyes opened and he could drink on his own from a little bowl. He was kept as warm as if he were with his mother and soon he grew into a rascal with a funny-looking head. Like any puppy he'd get confused: he wouldn't find his bottom to sit on, so he'd sit on his head instead, and when that would hurt, he'd wonder why. He wouldn't know what to make of his tail, so he'd chase it; he only knew how to count to two, so he'd get tangled in his four legs, and in the end he'd topple over, startled, showing his pink tongue that looked like a thin slice of ham. After all, every puppy is like, ah well, just like a little baby. Žanka and Ferda would have told you more about him—what trouble it was for them, old horses, always to be on guard for fear of treading on that silly dog. You know, my friends, a hoof is not a slipper; it needs to be lowered very softly, very gently so that a little creature on the ground doesn't squeal and whine in pain when stepped on. Children are trouble, that's what Žanka and Ferda would have told you.

Peanut grew into a really fine dog, happy and playful, just like any other. Yet, there was still something wrong with him. No one ever heard him bark or growl! All he managed was to squeal and to whine a little, but never to bark! Then one day Grandmother said to herself, "I'd like to know why this dog doesn't bark." She wondered about this for three days, walking around as if bereft of her soul. On the fourth, she said to Grandfather, "Would you know why our Peanut never barks?" Now it was Grandfather's turn to wonder. For three days he walked around shaking his head, and on the fourth, he said to Šulitka the horseman, "Do you know why Peanut never barks?" Šulitka took the question to heart. He went to the pub and pondered it for three days and three nights. When, on the fourth, he was finally ready to take a nap, his head was spinning. He called the owner over and pulled change out of his pocket to pay the bill. He kept counting the change, but the devil himself must have interfered, for he couldn't figure it out for the life of him. "Come on, Šulitka, didn't your mother teach you how to count?" asked the pub owner. At that, Šulitka stopped counting, tapped his forehead, and scurried off straight to Grandfather. "Master," he yelled at the door, "I've got it! Peanut doesn't bark because his mother never taught him how!"

"Well, I'll be . . . " said Grandpa. "You're right! Peanut never knew his mother and neither Ferda nor Žanka could ever teach him how to bark. There isn't another dog in the neighborhood . . . It certainly figures. Peanut can't even know what barking sounds like. I'll tell you what, Šulitka, you'll teach him how." So Šulitka sat beside Peanut in the stable and taught him how to bark.

"Ruff, ruff, listen to how it's done," he began. "First, you must say rrrrr, here, in the throat, and then, at once, you let it burst from your mouth. Ruff, ruff! Rrrr, ruff!" Peanut didn't know why, but these sounds were music to his ears. Suddenly, out of sheer joy, he barked himself. That first bark came out a bit peculiar, like the screech of a knife on a plate. Listen, all beginnings are difficult. You didn't know your ABC's immediately either. Ferda and Žanka listened and wondered why old Šulitka was barking. In the end they just shrugged their shoulders and lost all respect for him. Peanut had an enormous talent for barking and he was a fast learner! When he went out with the wagon for the first time, yip!—he barked to the right, yip!—he barked to the left, as if he were shooting a gun. To his very last day he never tired of barking. He barked the whole blessed day long. It gave him such pleasure to have learned it so well.

Driving with Šulitka and riding on the wagon wasn't Peanut's only responsibility. Every evening he would make the rounds of the mill and the yard to see that everything was in place. He yapped at the hens to stop cackling like old women at the market. He would stand before Grandfather, wagging his tail and looking cocky, as if to say, "Time for bed, Karl, I'll take care of everything." Grandpa would praise him and then, blissfully content, go to sleep.

During the day, with Peanut running along, Grandfather often made the rounds of the villages and small towns to purchase wheat and other odd stuff, maybe cloverseed or lentils, or perhaps poppyseed. At night, on their way home, Peanut wasn't a bit scared. He always knew his way home even when Grandpa, himself, wasn't quite sure about it.

One day, after Grandpa had bought some seed, let me see, where was it . . . it must have been in Evilville, I guess, he stopped for a moment at the inn. Peanut was left outside. While he was waiting for his master, something delicious tickled his nose. The smell from the kitchen was so luscious that Peanut simply had to peek inside. There, upon my soul, were people dining on sausages! Peanut sat down and waited to see if perhaps a casing would fall under the table. While he waited, Grandpa's neighbor (now quickly, what was the man's name? I guess it was Youdal, well, let it be Youdal) Youdal pulled his wagon up to the inn. When Youdal found Grandfather at the bar, one word led to another, and not long after, the two neighbors clambered into Youdal's wagon, ready to go home together. Grandpa had forgotten all about Peanut and the two men drove off. Meanwhile, Peanut sat in the kitchen, begging for sausages. After their meal, the diners tossed the sausage skins to the cat curled on the hearth and Peanut was left empty-handed. Then he remembered Grandfather. He looked for him, sniffing all over the inn, but Grandpa was gone. When the innkeeper noticed, he said, "There Peanut, look," pointing with his hand, "your master went that way." Peanut understood and set off for home by himself. At first, he trudged alongside the road, but after a while he said to himself, "I'm no fool. Why don't I take a shortcut over the hill." So he went over the hill and through the forest. Twilight came and night fell, but Peanut wasn't the least bit afraid. "I've got nothing anyone could steal," he thought.

As the full moon came into view and the trees by the forest path parted to reveal a glade, the moon loomed over the treetops and all was so beautiful that Peanut's heart leaped in awe. The forest hummed softly as if playing the harp. Peanut ran through the forest, which had turned into a jet black tunnel. Suddenly a silvery light glistened before him. The sound of harps became louder and every hair on Peanut's back bristled. He crouched close to the ground, staring in a daze. Before him, there unfurled a silver-bright glade where fairy dogs were dancing. They were splendid white dogs, almost translucent, and so feathery light that they didn't even disturb the dew on the grass. They were fairy dogs for sure. Peanut knew that at once because they lacked that interesting, faint scent by which a dog can tell a real dog from a fairy. Peanut lay down in the wet grass and stared until his eyes were ready to pop out. The fairies danced, scampered, and played with each other, chased their tails, so gracefully and airily that not a single blade of grass moved beneath them.

Peanut watched very closely, for if one scratched or bit for fleas he would know it was only an ordinary white dog, rather than a fairy dog. None scratched or bit for fleas, leaving no doubt they were fairies. When the moon rose high, the fairies lifted their heads and began to howl and sing softly and enchantingly. Not even The National Theater Symphony Orchestra could have made more beautiful music. Peanut was moved to tears. He would have joined in had he not been afraid of spoiling it all.

After concluding their chorus, they lay down around an old, stately dog who must have been a valiant fairy or enchantress, all white and serene. "Tell us a story," the fairies implored.

The old fairy dog considered and then said, "I will tell you how dog created man. When the Lord created the whole world and all the animals, he chose a dog to be their leader, for the dog was the best and the wisest of them all. In Paradise all the animals lived, died, and were born again happy and content, except dogs who grew sadder by the day. So the Lord asked the dogs, 'Why are you so sad when all the other animals rejoice?' The oldest dog spoke, 'You see, dear Lord, the other animals have no need of anything, but we dogs have brains that tell us some-

thing exists that's superior to us, and that's you, O Creator! We can smell everything but we can't smell you and we miss that terribly. Therefore, O Lord, grant us our wish and create a god we can smell.' The good Lord smiled and said, 'Bring me some bones, and I will create a god for you whom you can smell.' The dogs scurried in all directions, and each returned with a bone: a lion's bone, a horse's bone, a camel's bone, and a cat's bone. In fact, there were bones of all the animals except a dog, for no dog would touch another dog's flesh or another dog's bone. When the pile of bones grew large, God made man out of it, a god the dogs could smell. Since man is made of the bones of every animal except the dog, he shares with the animals all their qualities: the strength of a lion, the perseverance of a camel, the craftiness of a cat, and the magnanimity of a horse, but he doesn't have the loyalty of a dog. No, man doesn't have a dog's faithfulness!"

"Tell us some more," the fairy dogs pleaded again.

The old fairy dog pondered and then continued. "I will tell you how dogs got to heaven. You know that after people die, their souls go up to the stars. It so happened that not a star was left for the souls of dogs, and so they had to be placed in the ground for their eternal rest. It remained this way until the time of Jesus Christ. When he was flogged and his blood was spilled, a hungry stray dog came by and lapped up the blood. 'Mary in heaven,' exclaimed the angels, 'that dog has received the blood of our Savior.' 'If that's the case,' said God, 'we will take his soul to heaven.' He created a new star, and attached a tail as a pointer on the way for dogs' souls. Barely did the first dog's soul reach the star, than it became so boundlessly happy it began running and scampering about the sky like a dog in a park, and it wouldn't follow its path like the rest of the stars. Now, these dog stars that romp about in the sky and wag their tails are called comets."

"Tell us some more," begged the fairy dogs a third time.

"I'll tell you," began the old fairy dog. "Long ago, here on earth, there was a dogs' kingdom and in it a large castle. People envied the dogs for their kingdom and practiced sorcery until the dogs' kingdom and their castle sank deep into the ground. Now, if you dug in the right spot, you would get to the cave where the dogs' treasure is buried."

"What is the dogs' treasure?" asked the fairies eagerly.

"It's a hall of exceptional beauty," the old fairy said. "The pillars are made of the choicest bones, and none of the bones are gnawed, not a single one. They are meaty like a goose leg still attached to the thigh. Then there is a throne built of smoked meat, and leading to it are steps of the purest bacon slabs. The slabs are covered with meat hash a finger thick—" Peanut could stand it no longer. He scooted out to the glade, yelping, "Where is this treasure? Where is this dogs' treasure?"

There was no one to answer him. All the fairy dogs, even the old one, were gone. Peanut rubbed his eyes. All he saw was a silvery glade. Not a blade of grass had been trampled by the fairies' dance, not a dewdrop had trickled to the ground. Alone, the still moon glimmered over the beautiful glade, surrounded by the black wall of the forest.

Once Peanut remembered that at home at least some water-soaked bread was waiting for him, he ran home as fast as his legs could carry him. From that day on, every now and then, when Peanut walked over the grass fields or through the woods with Grandfather, he would remember the dogs' sunken treasure deep in the ground and he would dig ferociously with all fours, burrowing a deep hole in the ground.

It's very likely that Peanut shared his secret with other dogs, and they in turn surely told it to others, and they again to more dogs, for now all dogs, at one time or another, when they remember the sunken kingdom, do the same thing: they dig holes in the ground, sniffing them longingly, hoping for a whiff from the depths of the earth of the succulent throne of their long-lost empire.

The
Bird's
Tale

H ow would you children really know what birds talk about among themselves? You wouldn't, for they speak our language only in the early morning, at dawn, when you are still sound asleep. Later they have no time for chatter. You know, it is no small chore to peck a grain here, to grub a worm there or to smack a fly in the air. Performing all those feats, a daddy bird can flap his wings off while a mommy bird must stay home to care for her babies. Now you understand why birds have time to chat only at daybreak when they open the windows of their nests, air their featherbeds, and prepare their breakfast.

"Morning," halloos the blackbird from his nest in the pine tree to his neighbor, the sparrow who resides in the downspout. "It's time."

"Yeah, yeah," says the sparrow, "I must be off to filch, filch, filch, and pinch, pinch, pinch so there's enough fodder. Right?"

"Right, right," coos the pigeon on the rooftop. "Life's tough, brother. Hardly any grains."

"Correct, correct," intones the sparrow, rising from his tiny bed. "That's what the automobiles are doing to us. Remember the times when we had more horses around? Plenty of grain was strewn everywhere. And now? Now a car flies by and leaves nothing behind. Not a thing. Not a thing."

"Only stink, only stink," coos the pigeon. "Wretched life. B-r-r-r! Better give it up, friend! Always on the wing, circling in the ring, cooing. Time and time again, and all in vain, no gain to speak of. And barely a handful of grain. Blasted times!"

"You don't perhaps think that sparrows are better off, do you?" the sparrow ruffled up. "If I were alone, without a family, I'd have taken wing and made off already."

"Like that sparrow from Dejvice," tossed in the wren from the thicket.

"Dejvice?" mused the sparrow. "A chum of mine lives in Dejvice. Philip's his name."

"Wasn't him," said the wren. "The one who flew away was named Joey. A dowdy fellow, that one. Never even washed or combed properly but all day long he'd croak: 'Ah, what a boring, rotten sparrow's life! Starlings, storks, swallows, nightingales—they all vacation in the South in winter. They fly to the Riviera, maybe to Egypt. Only the sparrow must toil his whole life away in Dejvice. I'll put an end to this grind,' Joey the sparrow clamored. 'If a swallow from the Inn on the Three Corners can fly to Egypt, is there any reason why I can't? Well, that's exactly where I'll go as soon as I pack my toothbrush, my nightshirt, my tennis racket and tennis balls. I'll thrash Cochet, Koželuh, and Tilden. Just you wait! I've got quite a few tricks in my pocket already. I'll pretend to serve, and instead I'll fly up myself and when they strike at me, I'll volley and vanish. You bet, bet, bet! And when I've beaten them all, I'll marry a rich American, and then I'll buy the Waldstein Palace and there on the roof I'll build a nest, but not out of ordinary straw. No, sir! I'll build it out of rice grass, wicker, and rattan, and out of sea grass, horsehair, and squirrels' tails. Eat your heart out!' Thus the sparrow boasted, and each morning he fussed about how he was fed up with Dejvice and how he'd fly to the Riviera."

"Did he?" asked the blackbird from the pine tree.

"He did," said the wren in the thicket, and continued. "He only waited for Independence Day, to hear the military band—to which he was partial—and the morning after, he flew southward. Now as sparrows never fly south, they don't know the way. In fact, Joey had neither enough feathers nor enough money to stay overnight at an inn. You know, sparrows are the perennial proletarians, for they only flitter about the roofs all day long. In short, Joey, pinched and broke, without a single penny, barely got as far as Kardašova Řečice, and not a bit farther. Thus he was rather pleased when the village mayor approached him, and said amicably, "You moocher, you good-for-nothing, do you think we've got enough horse fritters here for every bum, every hayseed, vagrant, or renegade? If you want us to let you stay here, the main square is off-limits. No pecking in front of the inn or on the main road. That's reserved for permanent residents. The backroads are OK. The domicile allotted to you by court order is a wisp of straw in a little shed next to house number fifty-seven. Now sign the lease and get lost so I won't see you again!' Hence it came to pass that Joey the sparrow from Dejvice, instead of flying to the Riviera, got stuck in Kardašova Řečice."

"Is he still there?" asked the pigeon.

"To this day," said the wren. "My auntie who lives there told me about him. She said that the old croaker

mocks the local sparrows and clamors, 'How vexing, how weary to be a sparrow in Kardašova Řečice. What a humdrum place, without a single streetcar, well, maybe a few cars, but not a sports stadium, not much of anything.' Then he prattles on about how he wouldn't dream of dying of boredom there, that he's gotten an invitation to the Riviera and is only waiting until they send him money from home. He prattled and babbled so much about the Riviera that the local sparrows concluded they too would be better off somewhere else and they turned into sloppy good-for-nothings, passing their time chirping, peeping and twittering, just like all the rest of the sparrows around the world, and now all they do is jabber, 'It's better elsewhere, better, better!' "

"Yeah, I sure know some wacky birds around here," interrupted a titmouse from a hawthorn bush. "The one from that rich countryside around Kolín, for instance. This was a swallow who once read in the papers that here we never do anything right, but in America, brother, that's a whole different ballgame. In America, they've got experts in everything! All sorts of gab like that. Now that swallow got it into her head that she had to get to America to have a look, mind you. And she went."

"How did she do that?" the wren wakened.

"I don't know," said the titmouse. "Most likely by boat. And then maybe by airship. Who knows? She may have made a nest on the blimp's belly, or she may have taken a cabin with a window. Through the window she could have stuck her head out and spat too. To make the story short, she was back within a year, ranting about how she had been to America and how in America every-thing's different. 'C'mon,' she would say, 'there's no com-parison! What progress! There aren't even any larks there, and the buildings are so enormously tall that if a sparrow has a nest on the roof of such a building and an egg falls out, it keeps on falling for such a long time before it hits the ground that a baby sparrow hatches out on the way, grows, marries, has a slew of kids, ages and dies in blessed old age, so instead of an egg, an old dead sparrow drops flat on the pavement. That's how tall buildings are in America,' she claimed. She also said that everything in America is built of concrete, and she had learned how it was done, that all the swallows ought to come and see how to build a nest of concrete, not of mud as stupid swallows still do to this day.

"So all the swallows from far and wide flew in: swallows from Mnichovo Hradiště, from Čáslav and Přelouč, from Český Brod and from Nymburk, and even those from Sobotka and from Čelákovice. There were so many that people had to string nineteen thousand two hundred seventy-seven yards of telephone and telegraph

wires so those swallows had something to sit on. When all the swallows had gathered, the American swallow told them, 'And now, boys and girls, watch how Americans build houses, I mean nests, out of concrete. First, you pile up a heap of cement and another of sand. Pour some water over, make mush, and out of it you build a modern nest. Now, in case you have no cement, you won't be building your nest out of concrete, only of mortar. You make a mush of lime and sand, but the lime must be slaked. First I'll show you how to make quicklime.' Having said that, zap, she flew toward a building site where bricklayers were using slaked lime. There she picked a mote of lime and, flit, she was on her way back. But as her beak was moist, the lime began to slake, hiss, and burn. Startled, the swallow let the grain of lime fall, and cried, 'Now you know how to slake lime! Merciful heavens! How it burns!

Owwww, how it singes! Good grief, how it stings! Holy owl! Ouch! Mommeeee!' When the other swallows heard her bawling and howling, they didn't tarry, they merely flicked their tails and off they flew home. 'Away from this heat! That's all we need, to burn our beaks in the bargain.' That's why, to this day, swallows build their nests of mud, not of concrete, like the swallow from America tried to teach them.—Well, so it goes. And I, my friends, must fly off to do some marketing."

"Dear Mrs. Tit," Mrs. Merle, the blackbird, called, "when you're at the market, would you get me two pounds of earthworms, please? And make sure they're the nice long ones, would you? I've no time for shopping today. I must teach the kids to fly."

"With pleasure, my dear," said the titmouse. "I know the effort it takes to teach children to fly properly."

"But I bet there is something you don't know," said the starling from the birch. "You don't know who taught us, the grown-up birds, to fly. I'll tell you. I heard it from the Karlštejn raven. The one who flew here during the deep frost. That raven is already one hundred years old and he heard it from his grandfather who heard it from his great-grandfather who heard it from the great-granduncle of his grandmother on his mother's side, so it must be the sacred truth and nothing but the truth. Well then, sometimes at night, you can see shooting stars falling from the sky. You see, some of the stars aren't stars at all, they're golden angel eggs. As these eggs fall from such a heavenly distance, they become blazing hot and flare like fire. That's the most sacred of truths, for the Karlštejn raven said so. People call those eggs by a different name. Something like meter or monster or motor, well, something like that."

"Meteors," said the blackbird.

"That's it," the starling agreed. "Now back then, birds didn't know how to fly yet. They scuttled around like hens. When they saw one of those angel eggs falling from heaven, they decided to brood on it and see what would hatch. That's the truth, the raven said so. One evening, while they were talking, a glowing golden egg landed nearby, with a thump, right from heaven. They all hurried to the spot, with the stork in the lead, for his legs are the longest. The stork found the golden egg and took it into his claws, but as the egg was blazing hot it burned the stork's little feet. Unmindful of the pain, he carried the glowing egg to the birds. Then, plump! he hopped into the water to cool his feet. That's why, from that time on, storks have waded in water to cool their claws. That's what the raven told me."

"And what else did he say?" asked the wren.

"Then a wild goose came waddling by to hatch the scalding egg. As the egg was still scorching hot, the goose burned her belly and had to jump into a fish pond to cool off. That's why geese swim with their bellies in the water. Then one bird after the other sat on the egg to hatch it."

"A wren did too?" asked the wren.

"Yes, even a wren," said the starling. "All the birds of the world sat on that egg to hatch it, except the hen. When the hen was told it was her turn, she said, 'Tut-tut! What? You think I've got time? Cluck! I must scratch, I must peck, forget it. I'm no fool.' So she didn't brood on the angel's egg. When all the birds had taken their turn, a divine angel chipped his way out. When he emerged, he neither scratched, nor chirped, but flew straight to heaven, singing hallelujah, hosanna. Then he said, 'Birds, my dear friends, how am I to repay your love in hatching me? Let me offer you a gift. From now on, you shall fly like angels. Look, you have only to flap your wings like this and snap, you're flying! Now pay attention and let's do it together, one, two, three!' And when he said 'three,' all the birds began to fly, and so they do to this very day. Only the hen doesn't know how because she wouldn't brood on the angel's egg. All this is the holy truth because the Karlštejn raven said so."

"Now let's do it," said the blackbird. "One, two, three!" With that, all the birds flicked their tails, flapped their wings, and flew off, each after its own pursuit, each with its own song, as the holy angel had taught them.

The First
Robbers'
Tale

or

Of a
Pudgy Great-Grandfather
and the
Robbers

by

Josef Čapek

M y late great-grandfather was a woodchopper by trade and, occasionally, on the side, he would deal in horses and cloverseed. Even when he was in his ninety-eighth year, he was still, thank God, a jolly and active old fellow, round and ruddy like an apple, and so fat that in summer my great-grandmother would move him into the cellar for fear the heat upstairs would melt him away. In the cellar he would make himself comfortable, snooze, drink beer sweetened with sugar, and look forward to cooler weather.

When the sweltering summer came to an end, Great-grandfather would emerge again, waddle about his business, farm, supervise, manage, arrange and keep house, buy, sell, and hunt for things, nail, hammer, and carpet, sweat and grind, stamp his feet in boots and shuffle them in slippers, eat and drink zestfully—in short, considering his advanced age and venerable corpulence, he bustled about so charmingly that seeing him brought a smile to everyone's face. His, no doubt, was the most valiant paunch in the parish; and, yes, our parish was proud of him, too. There wasn't another like him in the whole parish: so heavy and ruddy, so broad-shouldered and wobbly, with such wrinkles around the eyes and such a round bulb of a nose and a double chin. No other parish had one like him either. When he arrived at the market in Hradec Králové, everyone, whether a student, a bishop, or a general, gazed at him. Now, a famished student or a dried-out general frowning like a herring, that, you would understand. But even the bishop wasn't by far so portly and ruddy, so burly and wobbling, so winsome as my late great-grandfather.

His face was clean-shaven, his nose and face were red, and his ears almost purple. Round his neck he'd tie a gaily colored kerchief; a stately vest arched over his paunch, with two rows of metal buttons, and a bulky tobacco case that held a pound of snuff at a time. There he would stand, among the carters, farmers, millers, and other fellows talking and lecturing; or, in case his legs gave him trouble, he'd sit in a tavern and talk, chatter, and crack jokes. Alas, such old-world, substantial people are all gone now! My great-grandfather lived through adventures so amazing and altogether remarkable that they don't happen any longer.

On his way home one day, with a couple of hundreds in his pocket from the sale of some horses, my great-grandfather and his dog Peanut were caught in the hills by a big storm.

Preferring beer to water, my great-grandpa right away looked for a tavern where he could safely wait out the downpour and thunder. There wasn't a house to be seen far and wide, except a forlorn and wretched inn, called At the Hanged Man and the Bottle. As the name hinted, the inn did not enjoy a good reputation. But as far as my great-grandpa could see, there wasn't another shelter, and as he was soaked to the skin and Peanut to the bone, he cursed the storm and trundled, panting, toward the inn where light shone in every window.

Neither my good great-grandpa nor Peanut had ever dreamed they'd run straight into a robbers' ball. That's right, the most evil robbers were giving a ball at that very inn, and all were dressed in costumes. Villainy, their leader, was cloaked in a tailcoat, complete with white tie and white gloves like a fine gentleman. His mistress, the cunning, powdered Coquette, was dressed like a ballerina; Cutthroat, the notorious murderer, was clothed in the powder blue and pink satin of a page; Archie Wag was there, and Bloody George, Snatcher and Cudgel, too, and so were the vicious Whittle, Dynamite, the international marauder, and Sly, the impostor—in short, it was a curious bunch, disguised as Turks, Chinamen, bears and drummers, organgrinders, knights and jugglers, well just as at any masked ball. They danced, feasted, and had a good time like perfectly decent folk. Only their eyes gave them away. Under their wigs, their hair bristled and their faces were scarred. Bloody George had two fingers missing but wore rings galore on the rest of them. The others' hands weren't workworn, yet they had large rawboned robber's knuckles and filthy nails, and some had dirty ears as well because all they thought of was mischief and forgot to wash properly with soap and hot water. They would barely pat their faces with a wet paw, just like a cat, and yet, they believed that was too much already. (Listen, children, when your mother tells you to wash your face in the morning, do so thoroughly. Remember what I am telling you.)

Well then, my great-grandfather was greatly surprised to have landed right at a ball. Though he was startled, he didn't immediately suspect robbers. Peanut snorted and shivered and he, I imagine, didn't suspect anything at all. So, Great-grandpa saluted with "Hi, hope you're enjoying yourselves," sat down to the side, and ordered a beer and Limburger cheese. Then one of the robbers, stuffing himself with cutlets and eating them with pickles, ice cream, and pastry in turn, said, "Enjoy your meal!" and my great-grandpa, who was particular about always being proper, answered, "Likewise." Now, when it dawned on those bandits that they had an honest fellow on their hands, their thoughts filled with mischief, and they decided to enjoy themselves at my great-grandpa's expense.

So they began. "Mister Swifty," twittered little Coquette mockingly, as if that were my poor great-grandpa's name. "Wouldn't the two of us make a nice couple! I'll put you down for a quadrille, a schottische, or even better, for a burlesque!" The robbers jeered. Coquette was skinny, too much so, actually, and what would Great-grandpa have done with a burlesque? He resented such brazen talk, and the laughter too. He was thinking of Great-grandma, and as I told you, Coquette was thin as a wisp. The girl certainly had nothing to brag about! Lifting his enormous boot full of hobnails and studs, Great-grandpa said, "I haven't got my patent leather shoes on and I might tread on your little foot, for your legs, dear Miss, as far as I can tell, look like pins, like matchsticks, now what am I saying, they look as if they belonged to a sparrow."

The answer didn't exactly please Coquette. Frowning, she turned toward her Villainy, the cruel robber. Ominously, Villainy yanked at his pencil-thin mustache. "You there, d'ya know where you are, you worthless rump of a boar? You're among robbers!" Great-grandpa got the jitters and began to sweat. Nothing good could come of this unfortunate encounter. "I am the famed Villainy," the chief went on, "this guy here with the lute, that's Cutthroat, the renowned murderer; and this Turk

here, that's the feared Whittle; the Chinaman, that's
bloody George; Dynamite is the bear; the drummer, that's
Snatcher; and the organ-grinder, well, that's Cudgel; Archie Wag's the juggler and Sly's the knight. My dear bloody
hatchet men! And this is our robbers' anthem," Villainy
said, and began to sing:

> "My friends, dear gentlemen,
> pals, chums, bloody hatchet men,
> swindlers, gamblers, pranksters,
> pilferers and gangsters,
> murderers, thugs and cheats,
> killers, blacklegs flush with deceit,
> we'll have a ball,
> join us one and all!"

Now it was Archie Wag's turn:

> "Chains o'gold, rings,
> precious stones—
> bingo! and all's yours!
> But if you fail
> you'll end in jail
> on gallows and gibbet, you bet!"

CHORUS:
> "Good riddance, farewell,
> we'll all be nabbed and hauled to jail,
> hot diggety hail!"

CUTTHROAT:
> "The gun's loaded,
> the knife's blade glistens,
> watch out, brother,
> beware and listen!"

CHORUS:
> "Good riddance, farewell,
> heed the advice,
> the slammer's waiting,
> we'll pay the price."

BLOODY GEORGE:	"Smite, stab, shoot and beat, yeah, they'll put the heat on you, mate, take heed, or you're dead meat!"
CHORUS:	"Adieu, farewell, fellows, we'll meet under the gallows."

The robbers sang and clinked their glasses at each chorus line while Great-grandfather froze in horror listening to the dreadful chant they sang so cheerfully. He was frantically trying to figure out what to do when it dawned on him that he too could spread some terror. He made his eyes bulge out, he furrowed his forehead, made an ugly face, and tried to lie. "I knew that all along," he said. "That's why I came. I too am in disguise. I am dressed as an old, fat woodchopper, but in truth I am Assassin, the famous robber, thief, and murderer. With these, my bare hands, I have stabbed and murdered, cut the throats of sixty men, thirty women, and fifteen children, and ransacked all the castles, forts, houses, buildings, and cottages in the area! And this here," Great-grandpa added, all the while looking around for Peanut, "is my police dog, the savage Sharpfang."

The robbers bellowed and sneered something awful. What else could they do? Peanut squatted quietly and meekly begged for a bone or two. Villainy lifted Great-grandfather's money pouch, his snuffbox, and even his colorful kerchief high in the air, everything the skillful Archie Wag had pulled out of Great-grandfather's pocket while he was bragging. "Well, look at this," jeered Villainy, "don't these belong to you? Isn't this your money, your snuffbox, and your tobacco that Archie pinched? If

you want to take from others and keep your own, you need
to apprentice with us, dear fellow."

Great-grandpa scratched his head, thinking, "I
won't get out of this mess easily, that much is clear."
"Yeah, we'll teach him!" roared the robbers. (Remember,
I've told you that they would make a fool of him and ruth-
lessly torment him, and then—well, who knows what else
they had up their sleeves.)

Sly began. "Tell me, rookie, who's got *his* in
someone else's pocket?" My great-grandfather thought
hard, and then said, "The one who's been robbed; what
was once his own is now in the pickpocket's pocket."
"Wrong!" Sly showed his teeth, "It's the thief! He's got his
hand in someone else's pocket!" Great-grandfather didn't
like the riddle at all. He saw he wouldn't get anywhere.
Had he said "thief," they would have laughed him off and
told him just the opposite, "the one who's been robbed."
They'd never let him guess right.

"Archie, tell him the qualities of a real thief!"
Villainy ordered.

Archie Wag strutted out in front of my great-
grandfather and began reciting, "A true thief, burglar, or
pickpocket must be black at night, green in grass, and
transparent in daylight. He must be thin as a wire and lim-
ber as an eel so that he can slip through the handle of a
mug, a keyhole, a doorcrack, or a crack in the wall. He
must be able to hide under a blade of grass breathless and
motionless, without sneezing or coughing. He must know
how to creep up the wall like a fly, his hands and feet must
be quiet like those of a cat, so the doors won't squeak, the

floor won't creak, the dog won't bark, and the master won't wake. He must not have more than a pound of bones in his body and only one and a half ounces of flesh, for he must be ready to slide into everything, penetrate everything, hide everywhere, meander through everything, and slip through everything. If he were heavier or fatter, he'd be hewed and hacked with an ax, shaped and trimmed with a knife, planed and filed, scraped, shaved, and rubbed, smoothed and scoured, stretched and bent, softened, sprung, and strengthened, threshed with a flail and stick, knocked into shape with a hammer, soaked, softened and dried, in water, under the ground, in fire and in the air."

Great-grandfather's hair bristled with terror, but now Snatcher stood in front of him, taking his turn. "What would you do, rookie, if, after you had broken into a house, someone awoke and cried from an adjacent room: 'Is someone there?' Then, what would you do?"

"I'd be quiet, I wouldn't make a peep," Great-grandpa answered.

"Wrong!" Snatcher laughed him off. "You'd answer, 'Nobody's here!' and yell it out loudly, so the one who just woke calms down and says, 'I'll be . . . and I thought someone was out there.' Should he cry, 'Robbers!' you must answer, 'I'm not stealing anything!' And if he screams, 'Mu-u-rdere-ers!' you must answer that you aren't being murdered, but are alive and well. And if he shouts 'He-e-elp!' you politely answer, 'Thanks, I'm getting along just fine.' "

"And now let's teach him how a genuine thief should get armed for burglary!" decided Bloody George.

"First, take your boots off, and hurry up or we'll do it for you," he ordered while aiming a pistol at my great-grandfather as if to show him that robbers who want to have fun mean business. All my great-grandfather could do was obey. So, sighing and groaning, he began to take off his muddy boots. What a chore that was! At home, of course, Great-grandmother always helped him, and when she couldn't manage by herself, the rest of the farm women would help too—old Šulitka's wife, and sometimes even Marie, and Anna, and even Rose. At other times even old Šulitka himself, and Mr. Zelinka would help him too. And now he must take the boots off alone! At last, the wretched boots were off, and Great-grandpa, panting, revealed his red and green striped socks that Great-granny had knitted for him that past winter.

"You need the boots off so no one hears you," said Sly.

Then they picked up the little board on which the innkeeper chalked up the debts, wrote on it "Nobody," and hung it on Great-grandfather's back.

"So no one sees you," grinned Dynamite.

Cutthroat then scooped some soot into his hands, and with it blackened Great-grandpa's face, and said, "So nobody recognizes you."

In the end, "to see well," they put into one of his hands a glowing robber's lantern, hanging on a twisted rope, so it kept spinning all the time, and "to have everything that he needs handy," they stuck into his other hand burglar's tools: hammers, axes, files, chisels, screwdrivers, augers, and picklocks. That's how the contemptible lot made fun of the poor old man. And worse was yet to come.

"Show us now how you'd sneak into a house on your tiptoes! Carefully, so the light of your burglar's lamp doesn't spin around and flicker, quietly, like a mouse, gently, like a snake, and lightly, like the tiniest fly! Hold your breath and stop at each step so that not a plank in the floor creaks, not a grain cracks, not a stalk rustles, not a sound is let out! For if the floor creaks, if the grain cracks and the stalk rustles and we hear one sound, we'll chip you and hack you with an ax; we'll cut you up and carve you out; with a plane and a file, we'll saw a bit off you; we'll thresh you with a flail, with a stick, and with a hammer; we'll soften you, bend you and toughen you, soak you, and dry you under the ground, in fire and in the air!"

Ice-cold shivers ran down Great-grandpa's back as he listened. But entirely at their mercy, he had to obey. The robbers formed a ring, as in a circus, looking forward to the performance.

"Get moving!" yelled Villainy.

Great-grandfather held his breath and strained to slink on his tiptoes. Alas! He was simply too heavy and waddling to maintain his balance. He tried to steal forward lightly and gracefully as if he were walking on eggshells, but at every step the floor creaked horribly, his knees cracked noisily, and he swayed and tottered as if he were walking on a tightrope. As he flailed with his arms, all the burglar's paraphernalia—the files, hammers, chisels, screwdrivers, and the picklocks, too—rattled tremendously. Sweat broke out on his forehead, and he moaned aloud while the robbers jeered and bellowed. (To hell with them, those miserable scoundrels, for laughing at old age and gray hairs!)

Suddenly, a tremendous noise flooded the place from outside: the clatter of horses, the rattle of coaches, the drone of cars, and the rumbling of planes. The robbers gave a start, and their laughter froze. While they had been making fun of my great-grandfather, they had completely forgotten to keep a lookout. And they had plenty to fear, the lot of them! The rumble stopped right at the inn. The robbers blanched. It could have been a general with his army, or a governor with his armed retinue, or maybe the police commissioner himself, with cops and bailiffs sent to encircle, arrest, and fetter the robbers with overwhelming force, and lead them to the gallows.

The robbers trembled with fear. It was too late to run away. Their eyes turned toward Villainy in desperation. And Villainy stood there, pulling on his remarkably long mustache, lost in thought. Then, he raised a finger of his right hand, tapped his forehead several times, and said, "I've got it! All of you stand still like statues! Don't move an inch till I give a wink! I'll take care of the rest!"

The robbers stiffened like statues. It was in the nick of time, for they could hear the steps draw ever closer.

The door opened and in walked not a general with his army, nor a governor, nor even the police commissioner, but the high and mighty Lord Havelock of London who had just happened to be passing by with his large retinue: his servants and footmen; chefs and cooks; his personal doctors and pharmacists; bodyguards, detectives, and policemen.

Lord Havelock was clearly taken by surprise at the sight of the motionless masked figures of a Chinaman, a ballerina, a Turk, a bear, a drummer, a juggler, a page,

and an organ-grinder. He halted in the doorway, fixed his monocle, scanned the place, and said, "Ah!" He continued with true English composure, "We were caught in the storm. I and my retinue intend to remain here until morning. Would you be the innkeeper?" The Lord addressed Villainy, who was eagerly bowing from behind a table.

"Your Lordship," bowed the exalted Villainy, "the innkeeper I am not. Allow me to introduce myself. I am Dumbaye, proprietor of the world-renowned traveling theater, the amazing panopticon, the mobile puppet show, at your service! Here are my puppets," Villainy pointed at the bewildered robbers. "Fifteen years I've worked on them, five years I've been improving them. Each puppet is full of wheels, hooks, and levers, all electrical, nothing's fake. Each is dressed differently, taught a different trick, all but indistinguishable from a living human. On my way to the most illustrious royal and ducal courts that had bestowed upon me numerous honors, orders, and distinctions, I, with my little theater, was held up here from the storm."

"Ah! And what can those puppets do?" asked His Lordship.

"Thank you for asking, Your Lordship," Villainy bowed obligingly. "I, Master Dumbaye, your humble servant, had not planned on staging a performance here, but I am endlessly honored by your gracious interest and, with your kind permission, I beg your leave to humbly present my theater to you in its entirety."

Lord Havelock put on his second monocle, and took a seat, surrounded by his entourage. Again, Villainy bowed deeply to the ground, and exclaimed, "A special performance for His Lordship Lord Havelock!" He straightened his coattails, and walked over to Coquette, who, in her ballet outfit, stood motionless, without blinking an eye, like a dummy in a store window. Villainy pretended to press a secret button on her back and cried, "A ballerina!" And lo and behold, Coquette—those cunning tricksters knew all the ropes—jerked her thin leg, raised her arm, put on a sweet smile, made a few ballet moves, turned gracefully around a few times; and after she had danced back to her place, she jerked her thin leg again, let her arm fall, and stopped, motionless.

"Ah!" said His Lordship. "How lovely!"

Villainy then approached Whittle, who was dressed as a Turk, pretended to press a secret button, winked at him, and exclaimed, "A Turk!" Lo and behold! Inside the Turk something rattled like a machine, then he jerked several times, crossed his arms on his chest, bowed three times, each time clearly enunciating the Turkish greeting, "Salaam Aleykum!"

"Ah!" marveled His Lordship, "that's lovely, too!"

Villainy then presented Bloody George, who wore the mask of a Chinaman. He too began rattling, jerked, raised two fingers, bowed three times, and three times uttered, "Chi chew hah, chiri miri ho!"

"Ah!" said His Lordship, "what a lovely Chinaman!"

That's how Villainy presented the complete show to His Lordship. Cutthroat plucked a little tune on the lute; Sly the knight knelt down, swore an oath, and thrice cheered, "Hurray!"; Archie Wag, in juggler's disguise, turned a somersault; Dynamite the bear growled and clumsily turned around; and accompanying all was Snatcher beating the drum, and Cudgel cranking the organ.

"Ah!" exclaimed His Lordship, "the puppets are beautiful! How much would you want for them, Sir?"

"Well, since it's you, Your Lordship, I'll let you have them cheap. Oblige me by setting your own price."

"One hundred thousand," resolved Lord Havelock. "My treasurer will settle with you tomorrow. And now, let me take the puppets with me to my bedroom. They will stand there."

Seeing Lord Havelock falling head over heals into his trap, Villainy was pleased to no end. What a splendid opportunity for the whole gang to kill His Lordship and cash in on the lordly booty!

"Your Lordship," Villainy bowed with cunning, "I am elated to know that my puppets will have the great honor of abiding in your revered proximity!"

Lord Havelock, vastly pleased with himself, was about to rise from his seat, when his eye fell on my great-grandfather standing in the corner in his striped stockings, his face blackened and a board hanging down his back.

"Ah!" wondered His Lordship, "and what does this puppet do, Master Dumbaye?"

Old Villainy had forgotten about my great-grandpa altogether and now, in a hurry, he couldn't think of a trick he could perform. He became all flustered and mumbled, "This one, er, well, this, er, is Nobody. How shall I—now, in fact, this puppet can't do anything yet. You see, I haven't quite finished it."

Now my great-grandfather wasn't born yesterday, and he decided it was his turn to play a trick on the robbers. Before Villainy could finish stuttering his reply, my great-grandpa began performing the part the robbers had taught him a little earlier. Out of the blue, in front of them all, he crept on tiptoes, like a thief. Villainy was struck dumb. His Lordship, in stupefaction, put on his third monocle, and exclaimed, "Ah!" and with him, his whole retinue went "Ah!" as well.

Moving stealthily like a thief, Great-grandfather first walked toward Snatcher, dove into his pockets, and began pulling out all the picklocks, screwdrivers, chisels, and augers, all of it, while singing the first verse of the robbers' anthem:

> "My friends, dear gentlemen,
> pals, chums, bloody hatchet men,
> swindlers, gamblers, pranksters,
> pilferers and gangsters,
> murderers, thugs and cheats,
> killers, blacklegs flush with deceit,
> we'll have a ball,
> join us one and all!"

"Ah!" uttered Lord Havelock and all his assemblage in unison. Sherlock Holmes, His Lordship Havelock's first private detective, pricked up his ears. He sensed something brewing.

Great-grandfather then walked to Archie Wag and began singing the second verse:

> "Chains o'gold, rings,
> precious stones—
> bingo! and all's yours!
> But if you fail
> you'll end in jail
> on gallows and gibbet, you bet!"

While he sang, he kept pulling out of Archie's pockets stolen jewels, trinkets of gold, bracelets, watches, and rings, eventually producing a stockpile large enough to open a jewelry business.

"Ah!" exclaimed Lord Havelock and his retinue. Stuart Webbs, His Lordship's second private detective, pricked up his ears. He was getting a hunch that something was brewing.

And Great-grandfather sang:

> "The gun's loaded,
> the knife's blade glistens,
> watch out, brother,
> beware and listen!"

all the while pulling from underneath Cutthroat's cloak tools of murder, knives, pistols, and daggers.

"Ah!" Lord Havelock and his entourage cried out. Joe Deebs, His Lordship's third detective, pricked up his ears. He felt in his bones that something was brewing.

So, my great-grandfather worked himself through the whole song and through the robbers, one after the other, unloading their tools, spoils, and murder weapons, displaying them all on the floor. Each time Lord Havelock went "Ah!" his company joined in, and Messrs. Higgs, Lutz, Leblanc, and Pitt, Lord Havelock's detectives, pricked up their ears in succession.

My great-grandfather left Villainy to the very end. Out of Villainy's pocket, Great-grandpa pulled his own money pouch, then the snuffbox, from which he took a goodly snuff on the spot, then his bright kerchief, into which he blew as if he were blowing an English horn, and sang:

> "Smite, stab, shoot and beat,
> yeah, they'll put the heat on you, mate,
> take heed, or you're dead meat!"

"It's Villainy!" exclaimed Clifton, one of Lord Havelock's detectives. He was now certain that they indeed were dealing with Villainy and his band of robbers. "Villainy!" exclaimed all the Lordship's detectives, bringing out ropes, fetters and handcuffs. "Villainy!" exclaimed

Lord Havelock, putting the fourth monocle into his eye. "Villainy!" cried out His Lordship's escorts, guards, and bailiffs, aiming their guns at the ringleader and his band.

"If you want to take from others and keep your own, you need to take lessons from me," my great-grandfather told the robbers.

Villainy, the robbers, and Coquette were handcuffed, led away, and brought to justice.

My portly great-grandfather put on his boots and washed, and Lord Havelock thanked him for having saved them from a monstrous fate. He presented my great-grandpa with many gifts, among them a beautiful tobacco case, stuffed with aromatic snuff which my great-grandfather, in turn, doled out to all the woodchoppers, horse dealers, and cloverseed traders in the area.

Great-grandfather called Peanut who, in the meantime, had been feeding on the leftovers from the robbers' feast and could hardly move. At home, my crabby great-grandmother greeted them peevishly, for she was convinced that their late homecoming was the result of a lengthy sojourn in a tavern. When my great-grandfather described to her all that had happened, she was happy that it all had come to such a good end.

The
Water
Sprite's
Tale

C hildren, if you believe that there are no water sprites, you are wrong. Why, there are so many different sorts and kinds, you wouldn't believe your eyes! Just to give you an example, I need only mention the one who lived near my hometown, in the river Úpa, under the sluice. Then there was the one in Havlovice who used to dwell near the wooden bridge, and there was yet another who resided in the Radec brook. That one was a German sprite who spoke not a word of Czech. Once he came to my father's office to have his tooth pulled and, in return, gave my dad a basket full of silver and pink pikes neatly covered with a nettle to keep them fresh. He was a water sprite, no doubt, for when he got up from the chair, he left a puddle on the seat. There was also the one next to my grandpa's mill, in Hronov, who kept sixteen horses under the sluice. That's why the engineers used to say that at that particular spot the river had sixteen horse-power. The sixteen white horses kept on pulling, the water mill went on spinning, and when one night our grandpa died, the water sprite quietly unharnessed the sixteen horses, and for three days the wheel stopped dead in its spokes. In large rivers there are water sprites who own even more horses, perhaps fifty, or maybe one hundred. On the other hand, there are also those poor ragamuffins who haven't even a wooden toy horse to play with.

Of course, a water sprite magnate in Prague, in the river Moldau, would be quite affluent, and a gentleman of fine standing. He might even own a motorboat and, in summer, he would vacation at the seashore. For in Prague, even an ordinary, second-rate water sprite has more money than there are shells in the sand, and he darts around in a flashy car spattering mud all around.

Then again, there are those petty little hucksters who barely have a puddle, no larger than the palm of your hand, and in it a frog, three mosquitos, and two water bugs; or their business is located in such a miserable trickle that if a mouse ran across it, he wouldn't even dampen his tummy. Some can barely lure a passing paper boat, and, if they are lucky, they may catch a baby diaper that the stream snatched from a mother while she was washing it. How awful!

Now the Rožmberk water sprite, for instance, has perhaps twenty thousand carp, as well as some scrod,

VODNÍK
PASE RYBY

catfish, mackerel, and toothy pike. There is no justice in this world, that's for sure!

Water sprites are loners by nature, but once or twice a year, during high tide, they will all gather and hold what you would call a district meeting. The ones who hail from our area always meet in the deep waters along Hradec Králové meadows, for there the country is nice and flat, with beautiful pools, backwater reaches, and river beds cushioned with the finest grade of mud. As is the case with liniment, the mud must be yellow or slightly brownish, for if it is red, or gray, it will not be supple enough.

119

What a lovely, dank place their conference ground is! There they sit and share the news: About the old water sprite George who was forced into moving from Hilldry because of some newly enforced regulation; about the price increase of pots and ribbon that was scandalous, to say the least! If a water sprite intends to make a catch, he now must spend thirty crowns on ribbons, another three on a small pot, and the pot turns out to be trash in the bargain. It would be better to quit the whole blasted business and take up a different trade altogether. They also talk about Faltys the redhead, from Jaroměř, who went into business selling mineral waters; and about the lame Slepánek who has become a plumber and makes water pipes; and about the others who made ends meet in different trades. Obviously, a water sprite can only take up a trade that relates to water: you understand that, of course, children, don't you? So, for instance, he can perfect any of the water crafts, become a waterman, and end up working on a ferry in, say, Waterloo. He can also grow watercress, water lilies, or watermelons. He may become a painter of watercolors. On the other hand, he can become a professional water polo player, too. He need not be well known, nor well-to-do, to pretend that he is well bred, but then again, he might be as well. At any rate, some water must be in it!

So you see, there are plenty of trades left open for water sprites. That's also why their numbers are dwindling. The roll call at every annual meeting is accompanied by sad comments, like "Again, we have lost five of us. If the trend continues, friends, our trade will slowly die out."

KOPANÁ
POD VODOU

"Times are changing," said the old Kreuzmann, the Trutnov water sprite. "Today is different from yesterday. Goodness, it must be thousands and thousands of years now since the whole of Bohemia was under water, and man, water man, to be exact, for people weren't around as yet. That's right, those were different times . . . darn it, where was I?"

"In Bohemia, under water," cued Greeney, the water sprite from Skalice.

"That's it," said Kreuzmann, and continued. "The whole of Bohemia was under the water, and Žaltman too, of course, and so was Red Mountain, and Crow Mountain, and all the other mountains, and any of you fellas could have crossed the country under water, I'd say from as far as Brno, to Prague, directly. Even Snow Mountain was hidden a fathom deep. Those were the days, my friends . . . "

"They were," recalled Kulda, the water sprite from Ratiboř. "And we weren't such loners and recluses then. We had underwater cities built of water bricks, furniture made of hard water, and featherbeds made of soft rainwater. We used hot water for heating our homes. And there was no bottom to the water, nor embankment, nor even surface. Only water and us."

"That's right," agreed Fox from Froggy Bottom marsh, nicknamed the Croaker. "And what gorgeous water that was! One could slice it like butter, roll it into balls, spin it into yarn, and twist it into ropes. Back then, water was like steel, like flax, like glass, like down. It was thick as cream, solid as oak, and warm as a fur coat. Everything was made of water. Goodness! Where can you find water like that today? Not even in America!" Croaker spat, then spat again, till he made quite a deep pool.

"It used to be . . . " Kreuzmann mused. "Water was absolutely beautiful, but it also was, how shall I put it? It was mute."

"How is that?" asked Greeney, who wasn't as old as the rest of them.

"What do you mean, how's that? It was silent," said Fox the Croaker.

"It had no voice. It couldn't talk yet. It was as quiet and mute as it turns now when it freezes. Quiet as midnight after the snow has fallen and not a thing stirs. When it's so still, so silently still you nearly quiver, your head popping out of the water, listening. When the endless silence wrings your heart—that's how quiet it was when water was mute."

"Then how come it isn't mute anymore?" asked Greeney, who was only seven thousand years old.

"Let me tell you," said Fox. "My great-grandfather said it happened some million years ago. There once lived a water sprite—what was his name, what was it? Reeds, no, it wasn't Reeds. Minařík, no, wrong again. Hampl, no not Hampl. Pavlásek, no it wasn't Pavlásek. Fiddlesticks! What was his name again?"

"Arion," said Kreuzmann.

"That's it, Arion," agreed Fox. "Arion was his name. I had it on the tip of my tongue. Now this Arion had a unique gift, a God-given talent of sorts. He spoke and sang so beautifully that he made your heart throb and cry with joy. What a musician he was!"

"Poet," corrected Kulda.

"Musician or poet, never mind," Fox replied. "He knew how to perform, let me tell you that. Great-grandpa said that this Arion needed only to hum the first measures of a tune, and everybody around him began to sob. He harbored a great grief in his heart, Arion. No one knows how great. Nobody knows what ill had befallen him, but his heart must have been broken to make him sing so beautifully and with such anguish. As he sang and wailed in the deep waters, every trickle quivered like a trembling tear, and as his song sailed through the water, every droplet caught a bit of its tune. That's why water isn't mute anymore. That's why it jingles and tingles, rustles and murmurs, trickles and bubbles, splashes, hums, drones, groans and wails, roars and booms, sighs, moans, laughs, plays as if on a silver harp, warbles like a nightingale, rumbles like an organ, blasts like a French horn, and speaks like a man in joy or in sorrow. Since that time, water has spoken all the many languages in the world and can say things so strange and wonderful that no one, man, least of all, understands them. Yet, before Arion taught the water to sing, it was mute as the sky."

"It wasn't Arion, though, who set the sky into the water," said the old Kreuzmann. "That happened later, during my father's time, Lord preserve his memory forever. Croakoax did it, out of love."

"How did that happen?" asked Greeney.

"I'll tell you how. Listen. Croakoax fell in love. He saw Princess Croakanne, and his heart was aflame. Croakanne was beautiful indeed. She had a yellow tummy, tiny frog's legs, a frog's mouth stretching from ear to ear, and she was all wet and cold. A beauty. There are none left like her."

"And what happened then?" inquired Greeney, eagerly.

"What do you think happened? Croakanne was beautiful and she was proud. She just puffed up, and said, 'Croak.' Croakoax went mad with desire. 'If you marry me,' he told her, 'I'll give you anything you wish for.' 'Then bring me the blue of the sky,' she said."

"What did he do then?" Greeney queried.

"What could he have done? He remained under the water and moaned, 'Croak, croaaaak.' He wanted to take his own life. To that end, he jumped from the water into the air, trying to drown in it. No one before him had jumped into the air. Croakoax was the first."

"And what did he do in the air?"

"Nothing. He looked up, and lo, blue sky was above. He looked down, and behold, blue sky was below, as well. Croakoax marveled. That happened at a time when no one knew that water reflected the sky. When Croakoax saw the blue sky in the water, bewildered, he uttered, 'Croak,' and fell into the water again. Then he took Croakanne on his back, and jumped with her into the air. Seeing the blue sky reflected in the water, Croakanne filled with joy and exclaimed, 'Croak, croak,' for Croakoax had brought her the blue from the sky."

"What happened then?"

"Nothing. They lived happily ever after and had oodles of tadpoles. Ever since, water sprites crawl out of the water to remind themselves that the sky is in their home. When one leaves home, whoever he may be, and looks back, just as Craokoax did when he looked into the water, he will understand that his home is there, where the real sky extends. The real, blue, beautiful sky."

"Who said so?"

"Croakoax did."

"Long live Croakoax!"

"Long live Croakanne!"

Just then, a man came walking by and thought to himself: "Boy, how the frogs are croaking today!" He grabbed a pebble and threw it into the marsh. The water sprites jumped in. They wouldn't have another meeting before the year was over. The water splattered high and splashed, then all was quiet.

The
Second
Robbers'
Tale

W hat I am about to tell you happened such an awfully long time ago that not even the late Zelinka—Lord bestow eternal glory upon him!— remembered it, and he after all remembered even my late, portly great-grandfather. It's been a terribly long time since the notorious and vile Villainy, the cruellest of murderers, with his twenty-one henchmen, fifty thieves, thirty pilferers, and two hundred underlings, smugglers, and fences held sway in the Brendy mountains.

He would lie in wait by the roadside, let's say by the road to Poříč, or perhaps to Kostelec, maybe even to Hronov, till some traveler, merchant, Jew, or a knight on horseback went by, and then he would ambush him and rob him of everything. The poor victim could consider himself lucky if Villainy had not stabbed, shot, or hung him from a tree, for such a brute and murderer he was.

Try to imagine a jolly old merchant driving down the road, calling to his horses, "Giddy-up" and "Whoahoo," and looking forward to a nice profit on the sale of his goods at Trutnov. It's true that while he drives through the forest, the thought of robbers frightens him a bit, but he hides his fear and whistles a lovely tune when suddenly out of the woods appears a fellow as tall as a mountain, broader than Mr. Šmejkal, larger than Mr. Jahelka, and two heads taller to boot, with a beard so thick he has a hard time finding his own mouth. Now when a rogue like this steps in front of the horses and yells, "Your money or your life," pointing a gun the size of a cannon at the poor old fellow, he of course has no choice but to hand Villainy all his money. Villainy in turn robs him not only of the carriage, the goods, and the horses, but also strips him of his coat, pants, and boots, and adds a few lashes with the poor man's own whip to make him speed home faster. I told you, Villainy was a vile fellow.

As there was no competition for miles around (the nearest highwayman operated around Maršov, but compared with Villainy, he was a bungler and an amateur), Villainy's business was booming. Soon he was wealthier than many a knight and even richer than a merchant. He had a little son and the old bandit resolved to send him to school. "And if it costs a couple of thousand, what the hell, I can afford it," he said to himself. "He'll learn German and French, so he'll know how to say 'pittshen' and 'jevoozaim.' He'll study the piano and know how to dance the schottische or the quadrille. He'll learn how to eat from a plate and blow into a handkerchief as is proper and re- spectable. I may only be a robber, but my son will be brought up a duke. Now I've said it, and that's that."

Then, he hoisted his son on the horse in front of him and off he went, tearing along the road to Broumov. There, in front of a monastery of the Benedictine fathers, he lifted the little fellow from the horse, and with his spurs clanking horribly, he thumped straight to the abbot. "I'll leave this boy in your care, Your Worship," he said. "Train him and teach him how to eat, how to blow his nose, how to dance, how to say 'pittshen' and 'jevoozaim,' well, all that befits a gentleman. Here, I'll leave this sack of ducats, marks, florins, piasters, rupees, doubloons, roubles, thalers, napoleondors, guineas, pieces of silver, Dutch guldens, and sovereigns. That should be more than enough for your troubles. Take care of my son, as if he were a little prince."

He turned on his heel and off he went back to the woods, leaving little Villainy in care of the Benedictine fathers.

So, little Villainy studied in that monastery with the holy fathers, alongside many princes, counts, and other rich young men. The portly Father Spiridion taught him how to say "pittshen" and "greasegott" in German, and Father Dominic crammed some French into his head, like "treysharmey" and "silverplay," and Father Amadeus coached him in all the courtesies, dances, and genteel manners. Mr. Kraupner, the choir director, gave him lessons in noseblowing, making it sound as delicate as a flute or as tender as an oboe, not like a bassoon, trombone, trumpet of Jericho, a piston, or an automobile, as was old Villainy's way. In short, young Villainy was taught the most refined manners and gallantries, as befit a true gentleman. In his black velvet suit with a lace collar he looked quite handsome, and he made himself forget that he grew up in a robbers' lair in the wild Brendy mountains and that his father, the old highwayman and cutthroat, went around in oxhide garb, smelling of horse manure and eating raw meat with his bare hands, as robbers usually do.

Briefly, young Villainy flourished with knowledge and elegance. Just as he was in the midst of his most beneficial studies, hooves thundered in front of the Broumy Abbey. A hairy henchman sprang from his horse, rapped on the gate, and when the brother porter let him in, he announced in a coarse voice that he was coming for young master Villainy, and that his father, meaning old Villainy, had summoned his son to his deathbed to take over the business. With tears in his eyes young Villainy bade farewell to the venerable Benedictine fathers as well as to all the young gentlemen and students. He followed the henchman to Brendy, all the while wondering about the type of business his father wished to bequeath him and resolving in his mind to carry it on with reverence, honor, and with exemplary courtesy toward all.

When they reached Brendy, the henchman led the young master to his father's deathbed. Old Villainy lay in an enormous cave on a bale of untanned oxhide, covered with a horse blanket.

"Hey, Vince, you lazy bum," he uttered heavily, "did you bring that lad of mine at last?"

"Dear Father," exclaimed young Villainy, kneeling down, "may the Lord find it in His heart to preserve you for many years for the pleasure of your neighbors and the ineffable pride of your descendants."

"Slowly, m'boy," said the old robber. "I'll be leaving for hell today, and I've got no time for your cooing. I reckoned I was to leave you a fortune big enough to live on without having to work but, damn it, this trade of ours has gone through terrible times the last few years."

"Dear Father," sighed young Villainy, "I had no inkling that you were suffering hardship."

"Well," grumbled the old guy. "I've got gout, you know, and I can't venture far from here. The merchants, those tricksters, they avoid the nearby roads. It's about time someone younger took over my job."

"Dear Father," said the young man ardently, "I swear to you by all that's dear to me that I shall take over your business, and I will conduct it honorably, with goodwill and friendliness to all."

"Well, I don't know how you'll fare with friendliness," mumbled the old man. "I, for one, stabbed only those who showed resistance, but compliments, my dear son, I haven't paid to anybody. You see, it somehow doesn't suit my line of business."

"And what is your profession, dear Father?"

"Robbery," uttered old Villainy, and passed away.

Abandoned, his young son was crushed to the bottom of his soul by his father's death and by the oath he'd sworn to carry on as a highwayman.

Three days after his father's death, Vince, the hairy henchman, came to report that nothing was left to eat and they'd have to go back to work.

"My dear fellow," begged young Villainy, "need it really be so?"

"You bet," Vince groused. "No Benedictine Father will bring you a stuffed pigeon here, I'm tellin' ya. If you want to eat, you'll have to work."

Without further ado, young Villainy pulled out a fancy pistol, mounted his horse, and headed toward the road, say to the road near Batňovice. There he lay in wait, figuring he'd rob anyone who went by. Barely an hour passed, and behold, an itinerant linen dealer, carrying his wares to Trutnov, appeared on the road.

Young Villainy stepped out of hiding and doffed his hat in a deep bow. Surprised at the sight of such a handsome young man, the linen dealer took his hat off as well, saying, "Greetings, young man."

Villainy came closer and again doffed his hat. "I beg your pardon," he said, "I hope I'm not inconveniencing you."

"Good Lord, no," exclaimed the linen dealer. "Is there anything I can do for you?"

"I implore you, dear sir, do not become frightened. I am Villainy from Brendy, the formidable robber."

A sly fellow, the linen merchant was not a bit afraid. "You don't say!" he said cheerfully. "So you are a colleague of mine! You see, I am a robber as well, the bloodthirsty Čepelka from Kostelec. Surely you know me!"

"I've not had the honor," apologized Villainy, bewildered. "This is my first time on this road. As it happens, I have just taken over from my father."

"I see, old Villainy from Brendy. That's an old, renowned robbery firm. Very well established, Mr. Villainy. My congratulations," remarked Čepelka, the merchant. "You ought to know that your late father and I were very good friends indeed. Just the other day, as a matter of fact, when we ran into each other, your dad said to me, 'You know, Čepelka, you hoodlum, since we're neighbors and colleagues, why not share the turf amicably. Here, this road from Kostelec to Trutnov will be yours and yours alone for the holdups.' That's what he said, and we shook hands on it."

"I beg your pardon a thousand times," young Villainy apologized. "In all honesty, I didn't know that this was your district. I regret deeply having set foot here."

"Well, let it pass this time," said the wily Čepelka. "Let me tell you though that your father also said: 'And I tell you something else, Čepelka, you ruffian. If you ever but smell me or any of my men around here, you can take his gun, cap, coat, anything, to remind him that this road is yours.' That's what your old man said, and he gave me his hand on it.'

"If that's the case," said young Villainy, "I must beg you most respectfully to accept this inlaid pistol, my beret with a real ostrich feather, and my jacket of English velvet as a souvenir, as a token of my deep respect as well as of my regrets for having caused you such inconvenience."

"All right then, hand them over and I'll forgive you," Čepelka replied. "But don't let me see you here again, young man. Now, giddy-up, horsie! Goodbye, and God bless you, Mr. Villainy."

"God be with you, m'lord, so noble and paternal," young Villainy called after him, and he went back to Brendy, not only without any loot but without his own coat. Vince the henchman bawled him out and ordered him to stab and rob the very first person he met on the road the next day.

So the day after, young Villainy lay in wait on the road near Zbečník, this time with his slender dagger ready in its sheath. It wasn't long before a carter with an enormous load approached.

Young Villainy stepped out and called, "Sorry, sir, but I must run you through. I beg you to get ready and say your prayers."

The carter fell to his knees, prayed, and wondered how to get out of this pretty mess. He said the first and the second Paternoster, and still no clever idea dawned on him. He was already on the tenth, then on the twentieth Paternoster, and still nothing.

"Now then sir," young Villainy cried, striking a fierce pose, "are you prepared to die?"

"Oh no!" squealed the carter, his teeth chattering. "Terrible sinner that I am, I haven't been to church for thirty years, I've sworn like a pagan, I've cursed, I've played poker, and sinned at my every step. If only I could confess at Polička, maybe the lord would forgive me my sins and wouldn't cast my soul into hell. I'll tell you what, I'll dash to Polička, and when I've confessed I'll come back, and then you can stab me."

"That's fine with me," agreed Villainy. "While you're gone, I'll wait near your wagon."

"Sure, but be good enough to let me have your horse so that I can return sooner."

Chivalrous Villainy agreed to that as well. Thus the carter mounted Villainy's horse and dashed off for Polička while young Villainy unharnessed the carter's horses and let them graze in the pasture.

The carter, trickster that he was, didn't go to Polička at all but stormed the nearest pub, announced that a highwayman was waiting for him on the road, had a drink to muster some courage, and with three patrons went after Villainy. The four men pummeled poor Villainy dreadfully, chased him into the woods, and the gallant robber returned to his cave not only without the goods, but without his own horse, to boot.

For the third day Villainy lay in wait, this time on the road to Náchod, to see what prey chance would bring. A small cart covered with an awning appeared, carrying nothing but gingerbread cookies to the market. Again, young Villainy stepped forward and yelled, "Man, give yourself up, I am a robber," just as Vince the hairy henchman had instructed.

The wagon stopped, the driver scratched his ear, then lifted the awning and said to someone inside the cart, "Mother, do you want to see a dandy robber?"

The awning parted and out of the little cart crawled a fat old hag, who put her hands on her hips and yelled, "You Antichrist, you archvillain, you bandit, you brigand, you cacodemon, you cannibal, you devil, you deuce, feral fiend, Goliath, heathen, hackney, hoax, how dare you hold up honest, decent folks?"

"My apologies, madam," whispered Villainy, mortified. "I had no idea there was a lady in the carriage."

"You bet there was, and what a lady!" the market woman ranted on. "You idiot, you ignoramus, you jerk, Judas, knave, Lucifer, you leech, you marauder, you murderer!"

"I beg your forgiveness a thousand times for having frightened you so," Villainy apologized, totally nonplussed. "Treysharmay, madammmme, silverplay, I assure you in my humblest compunction that—that—"

"Off with you, you slug," hollered the venerable lady, "or I'll tell you what you are, you heathen, inhuman, deformed, godless, light-fingered pickpocket, pirate, robber and rake, you rogue, satan, slouchy slob and snake, you trickster, Tartar, you ugly mistake, you—"

More of it young Villainy did not hear, for he took to his heels and did not stop until he reached Brendy; and even there it seemed that the wind carried words that sounded something like: "—vicious, vile, wicked, worthless, wretched, yahoo, yo-yo, zwieback—"

Well, that's what always happened. Near Ratiboříce, the young robber held up a gilded chariot, but as the coach carried a princess, and she was very pretty, Villainy fell in love with her and only took a scented kerchief, and that, actually, the princess gave him for asking. You may well imagine that out of that scent his gang on the Brendy mountains didn't get much of a meal.

On yet another occasion, at Suchovršice, he held up a butcher who was taking a cow to the slaughter house at Úpice. Villainy was about to kill him, but the butcher begged him to tell his twelve orphans things so touching, highminded, and moving that Villainy sobbed with compassion and let the butcher go. The butcher, an old rascal, left not only with the cow, but with twelve ducats that Villainy made him take with the promise that he give each of his twelve children a gold coin as a souvenir from the horrible Villainy. The old fox, a bachelor, didn't have even a cat, let alone twelve children. What is there to say? Every time Villainy intended to murder or rob, something always appealed to his benevolence and sympathy, so that he not only didn't take anything from anyone, but gave away everything he had.

Clearly, in that fashion his business didn't prosper. His underlings ran away and took up honest work. Vince the hairy henchman enrolled as apprentice at the Hronov mill that to this day stands down the hill from the church. Young Villainy was left alone in the cave at Brendy, hungry and at wit's end. At last, he remembered the Benedictine Abbot at Broumov who had loved him so very dearly, and he set out to ask him for advice.

When Villainy got to the Abbot, he knelt and wept and told him about the sworn oath he'd given to his father that he'd be a robber, but since he was brought up with courtesy and kindness, he could not, for the love of the world, either kill or rob anyone against his will. What was he to do?

The Abbot snuffed his tobacco twelve times, and twelve times he fell into deep thought. Finally he said, "Dear son, I commend you for being so polite and kind to your fellow men. You cannot, however, remain a robber, partly because it is a mortal sin, and partly because you don't have the knack for the job. Now to keep the oath you gave your father, you must go on holding people up, but from now on you'll be doing an honest job. You'll collect the toll on one of the roads. You'll hold up every driver and charge him two pennies. That's what you'll do. In that job you can be as courteous as you wish and as polite as you are able."

The Abbot then wrote a letter to the chairman of the County Council in Trutnov, interceding on behalf of young Villainy, humbly requesting for him the job of a toll collector. Villainy carried the letter to the County Council in Trutnov and was assigned a road leading to Zálesí. That's how it came to pass that the gallant robber became a toll collector, holding up wagons and carriages, collecting in all honesty two pennies for the passage.

Many years later, the Abbot from Broumy traveled in a coach to visit the curate in Úpice, looking forward to meeting the gallant Villainy and also wanting to see how he was getting along at the tollgate in Zálesí. As it happened, at the tollgate, a mustached man—it was Villainy himself—approached the coach and, mumbling something, stretched out his hand.

The Abbot reached into his pocket, but as he was rather stout, he had to hold his belly up with one hand to get the other into his trouser pocket, so it took a little while to get the money out.

Villainy bawled him out in a rough voice, "Move along, will ya? How long d'ya think I'll wait for the bloody two pennies?"

The Abbot fumbled in his coin purse. "Sorry, young man," he said, "I seem not to have any pennies. Would you mind giving me change for a quarter?"

"Go to hell," Villainy yelled, "if you don't have change, what the hell are you doing here? Give me two pennies or get lost!"

"Villainy, Villainy," rebuked the Abbot woefully, "don't you recognize me? What happened to your courtesy?"

Villainy was taken aback, for only now did he recognize the Abbot. He muttered something very nasty but then pulled himself together and said, "Don't be so surprised, Your Worship, that I'm not as polite as I used to be. Has anybody ever seen a toll collector, an inspector, a tax collector, or an executioner who isn't at least a little bit of a grouch?"

"That's true," the Abbot replied, "nobody ever has."

"You see," snarled Villainy, "and now go to the devil."

That is the end of the tale about a gallant robber. He may be dead, but his offspring are all around us. You can easily recognize them, for they are always ready to harass people without the slightest provocation. And that's a sad state of affairs.

The
Tramp's
Tale

T here once lived a poor, penniless man, truly a pauper. His name was Francis King, but no one called him that, except when a cop booked him for loitering; at the station, they would enter his name into a thick book and let him sleep on a cot. In the morning they told him to leave. Though at the police station they may have correctly called him Frank King, the rest of the world referred to him by far less favorable appellations: that tramp, hobo, loafer, vagrant, slapdash, that ragamuffin, bum, lazy-bones, poor devil, that individual, outlaw, scoundrel, vagabond, hoodlum, good-for-nothing, that rabble-rouser, riffraff, ragtag, as well as numerous other names. If every name were worth a mere crown, it would have paid for a pair of yellow boots and perhaps even a hat that he could have bought, but as it was, he had nothing and existed only on handouts.

Needless to say, Frank King did not enjoy the best reputation, but to tell you the truth, he was merely a tramp stealing time from the good Lord (who, however, has so much time in eternity that not a bit of it disappears) and whistling on the whittle. Now do you know what whistling on the whittle means? I'll tell you how it's done: in the morning, let your mouth dry out; at noon, don't have a bite; in the evening, instead of eating, pick your teeth and when your stomach starts rumbling, you'll be whistling on the whittle. Frank King was so good at whistling on the whittle he could have given concerts. There wasn't much to him, poor fellow, still what there was was good through and through. When he received a chunk of bread, he ate it, and a nasty word he swallowed too, so great was his hunger. When he remained empty-handed, he would lie down somewhere behind a wooden fence,

swaddle himself with darkness, and beg the stars to keep
an eye on his cap so nobody would steal it.

Such a tramp knows many a thing about the
world around him. He knows where he'll get a bite and
where he'll collect insults. He knows where the bad dogs
are that hate tramps more than they dislike cops. Let me
tell you, there once was a dog, quick, what was his name?
Yeah, Foxl they called him. He too has gone to meet the
angels, poor fellow. Now, that Foxl, the dog of the manor
in Chýže, was an eccentric. He would spot a vagrant and
immediately he'd yelp with joy, dance around him, and
lead him straight to the manor kitchen. But when a big
shot came calling, say a baron, a count, a prince, or the
archbishop of Prague himself, Foxl would bark like crazy,

and he would have torn the caller to pieces if the coach-man hadn't quickly locked him up in the stable. You see how different dogs are, one from the other? So, when it comes to people, well . . .

Speaking of dogs—do you know, children, why dogs wag their tails? I'll tell you. When God created the world and everything in it, he went from one living crea-ture to the next inquiring about their well-being, affably asking whether things were to their satisfaction, whether they lacked anything, and questions like that. So he came to the first dog in the world and asked him if there was anything he needed. The dog was about to shake his head in a hurry, to show, thank God, that he needed nothing at all, when he caught the smell of something mighty inter-esting. Perhaps it was the first bone or the first sausage casing, still warm from the hands of the creator, but in any case, he became all confused and eagerly wiggled his tail instead. Ever since, dogs have wagged their tails while other animals, such as horses and cows, have known how to shake their heads like people. Only the pig can neither nod nor shake his head. When the Lord asked him whether he was satisfied in this blessed world, the pig went on bur-rowing for acorns with his snout and wagged his tail in irritation, as if he were saying, excuse me, wait a moment, I've got no time right now. Since then, while alive, pigs wiggle and twitch their tails, and for punishment, to this very day, their tail is always eaten with horseradish or mustard, burning the pig even after his death. That's how it has been since the world's creation.

But that's not what I wanted to talk about today. I wanted to tell you about a tramp whose name was Frank

King. Now that tramp roamed around the world getting as far as Trutnov, where the Germans live, and also to Hradec Králové and to Skalice, and even to Vodolov and to Maršov and other far away cities. At one time he worked for my grandfather in Žernov, but a tramp is a tramp, after all. He picked up his bundle and moved on again, this time to Starkoč or to some other far corner of the world. He was neither seen nor heard of again—that's how restless he was.

I have already told you that people would call him hobo and ragamuffin and bum and other names as well. Now at times they would also call him a filcher, a thief, a rogue and marauder, but they were doing him a great injustice, for Frank King never took, stole, nor pinched a thing from anyone, not as much as the dirt behind his nails, on my word. That's exactly why, in the end, by virtue of his honesty, he achieved great fame. It is about that very matter that I want to speak.

One day, Frank the tramp found himself in the market town of Podměstečko, deliberating on whether to go to the Vlček for a bread roll or to stop at the old Prouza for a muffin, when along came a fine gentleman. He may have been a foreign businessman or perhaps a traveling salesman because he carried a leather case in his hand. Suddenly, a gust of wind blew the man's hat off and set it rolling down the road. "Hold this for a minute, will you?" the man shouted, and tossed the case to Frank the tramp. Before you could utter a word, the man had disappeared in the dust, chasing his hat.

Frank King stood with the case in his hand, waiting for the gentleman to return. He waited half an

hour, then an hour, but the man was gone. Frank didn't
even dare slip away for that dinner roll, lest the gentleman
might miss him when he returned for the case. He waited
two hours, then three, and to drive away the boredom, he
began whistling on the whittle. Still, the man didn't return, and night began to fall. Stars glittered in the sky, the
whole town was asleep, curled up like a cat on a hearth-
stone pillow, softly purring. How good it felt to be tucked
in the feather bed! Frank the tramp was still standing by
the roadside, numb, looking at the stars and waiting for
the gentleman.

Right at the midnight chime a terrible voice from
behind him resounded, "What are you doing here?"

"Waiting for a stranger," Frank said.

"And what have you in your hand?" asked the
awful voice.

"It's a case that belongs to the gentleman," the
tramp explained. "I must keep it until he returns."

"And where is this gentleman?" queried the
voice for the third time.

"He ran off after his hat," Frank answered.

"Uh-huh, I see," said the dreadful voice.
"Sounds suspicious. You'd better come with me."

"That I can't do," the tramp objected. "I must
wait here."

"In the name of the law, I am arresting you,"
roared the powerful voice. Then it dawned on Frank King
that the voice belonged to Mr. Boura, the policeman, and
that he'd better obey. So he scratched his head, sighed, and
away he went, to the police station with Mr. Boura. There,
they entered his name in a thick volume, locked him up in

the slammer, and put the case under lock and key where it would stay until morning when the judge returned.

In the morning, they brought the tramp in front of the judge. Wouldn't you know it, it was Mr. Šulc, the magistrate himself—he too is free of headaches in the next world.

"You good-for-nothing, you slipshod, you rascal, you," said the judge. "You're back again? It hasn't even been a month since you were locked up for loitering. Good grief, man, you're a nuisance! They've got you in for loitering again?"

"Oh no, Your Honor," said Frank the tramp. "Mr. Boura took me in for standing still."

"You dimwit," the judge said, "why were you standing still? If you hadn't been standing still no one would have nabbed you. Also, I heard something about a briefcase. Is it true?"

"Yes, Your Honor," answered the tramp. "A stranger gave me that briefcase."

"Sure, sure!" the judge exclaimed. "We've heard that story before! A man steals something, and says it was given to him by a stranger. We've heard that one before. Try something else. So, what's inside this case?"

"Now that, I swear, I don't know, Your Honor," said Frank the tramp.

"Sure you don't, you trickster," said the judge. "We'll see for ourselves."

With that, the magistrate opened the briefcase. He started, bewildered, for the case was full of money. When he'd counted it all, it came to one million three hundred seventy-seven thousand eight hundred fifteen crowns and ninety-two hellers, and there was a toothbrush too, tossed in for good measure.

"Good Lord! Where did you steal this?"

"If you please, Your Honor, the stranger who ran off after his hat had asked me to watch it for him," maintained Frank King.

"Oh, you thieving rascal," bellowed the judge, "you don't think I'm going to buy this, do you? I'd like to see the man who would entrust a ragamuffin like you with one million three hundred seventy-seven thousand eight hundred fifteen crowns and ninety-two hellers, and a toothbrush besides! To the dungeon, march! You needn't worry, we'll find out whose case you robbed!"

So, it came to pass that they locked poor Frank up in the dungeon for a very long time. Winter ended, spring too had passed, and still they could find no one to claim the money. So His Honor, Magistrate Šulc, and Mr. Boura, the policeman, and the other gentlemen of the court and the police began to think that Frank King, a tramp without a shelter and without a steady job, a repeated offender and a rude mischief-maker, had robbed a case of money from a stranger, and then buried him somewhere.

A year and a day went by, and Frank King stood trial for murdering a stranger and for robbing him of one million three hundred seventy-seven thousand eight hundred fifteen crowns and ninety-two hellers, and a toothbrush, to boot. Dear children, the punishment for a crime like that is hanging.

"You lout, you thief, you scum," the judge addressed the defendant, "for God's sake confess and tell us

where you killed and buried the man. You'll hang easier if you confess."

"But I didn't kill him, Your Worship," poor Frank maintained. "He only ran after his hat, and was off and gone in a flash. I didn't have time to bat an eyelid. The briefcase . . . well, in a manner of speaking, he gave the case to me."

The judge sighed. "If you insist, we'll hang you without confession. Mr. Boura, go ahead and hang that mulish felon. God help you."

He had hardly finished speaking when the door flew open and there stood a stranger, all covered with dust and panting. "It's been found!" he proclaimed.

"What's been found?" inquired the judge in a stern voice.

Okresni soud.

"The hat," said the stranger. "Was that a run-around! A year ago, to this day, I was walking down the main road when, suddenly, the wind blew my hat off. I threw my suitcase to someone, I haven't the slightest idea who, and I tore after the hat. The hat, the little rascal, rolled over the bridge to Sychrovo, and from there to Zálesí and to Rtyně, and through Kostelec to Zbečník, and across Hronov to Náchod. It rolled all the way to the Prussian border and still the chase continued. I had nearly caught it, when, at the border, I was caught by a customs officer who grilled me about my running. 'I am chasing my hat,' I told him, but by the time I got through to him, my hat was gone again. So I had a night's rest, and in the morning, I set out to track my hat through Prussia, to Lobau, and then to Görlitz, with the ill-smelling springs—"

"Wait!" the judge interrupted. "This is a court of law, not the geographical society."

"I'll cut it short," said the stranger. "In Görlitz I found out that my hat had drunk a glass of mineral water, had bought itself a walking cane, and had boarded a train for Schweidnitz. Needless to say, I followed. In Schweidnitz, my hat, that scamp, slept in a hotel, didn't pay the bill, and left, with no forwarding address. After numerous inquiries, I learned that it was staying in Kraków, and that it had even proposed to a widow. So I followed it there."

"And why, pray tell, did you chase it?" wondered the judge.

"Well, that hat was as good as new," said the stranger, "also, I'd slipped the return half of my train ticket to Starkoč under the hatband. It was the return ticket I wanted, Your Honor."

"That's reasonable, I'd say," the judge stated.

"I'd hope so," said the stranger. "After all, you wouldn't pay for the same ticket twice, would you? Now where was I? Aha, on my way to Kraków. All right, I arrived in Kraków but, in the meantime, my hat, that rascal, had departed for Warsaw, pretending to be a diplomat."

"That's fraud," exclaimed the judge.

"Well, that's the reason I reported it, too," said the stranger. "The police wired an arrest warrant from Kraków to Warsaw but, meanwhile, my hat had purchased a fur coat, for winter was setting in. It grew a beard and left for Moscow."

"What did it do in Moscow?" asked the judge.

"What would you expect? It got involved in politics, that little wretch, became a journalist, and later decided to seize power and overthrow the government. By that time, the Russians had already seized it and sentenced it to death by firing squad. As they led the hat to the execution grounds, a gust of wind blew up, and my hat, that street urchin, began to whirl, slipping between the legs of the soldiers, and rolling across mother Russia to Novocherkassk. There, it donned a fur cap, and became the chief of the Tartars. I still kept chasing, and finally, I caught up with it. And what do you think my hat did, the scoundrel? It whistled for the Tartars and ordered them to shoot me!"

"What happened then?" asked the judge eagerly.

"What do you mean what happened? I told them that we are not afraid of Tartars, and we chop them up into tartar sauce. Have you ever had tartar sauce, Your Honor?"

"Often, with fish," replied the judge.

"Well, I also told them that they would be pounded into cream of tartar, and whipped into egg whites. That was enough to scare them out of their wits, so they let me go. However, my hat, the rascal, had mounted a horse and darted eastward. I, of course, scurried after. In Orenburg, my hat boarded the Trans-Siberian railroad heading for Omsk, but in Irkutsk I lost track of it. I understand that somewhere around there it came into money, but was robbed by marauders and barely came out alive. I ran into it on a street in Blagovyeshchensk, but it slipped away from me, the sly fellow, and rolled across the

whole of Manchuria to the China Sea. There, on the shore, I caught up with it, for my hat was afraid of water.''

"So you caught it there?" queried the judge.

"Nothing of the sort," said the stranger. "I ran toward the seashore, but just then the wind turned westward and my hat turned with it. I ended up chasing it across China and Turkestan, partly on foot, partly carried on sedan chairs, and partly on horseback and on camels, until in Tashkent it got on a train back to Orenburg. Then to Charkov and Odessa, from there to Hungary, where it took a turn toward Olomouc, Česká Třebová, Týniště, and at last it returned home again. Why, only five minutes ago, I caught it in the market square as it was having a bite in the inn. Here it is."

With that, he displayed the hat. It was ripped to shreds. Surely nobody would take it for such a rolling trickster.

"And now, let's see whether that return ticket is still stuck under its ribbon." He slid his hand behind the hatband and pulled out the ticket. "It's here all right," he cried triumphantly. "Now at least I can travel back to Starkoč without having to pay the fare twice."

"But my friend, that ticket is no longer valid," said the judge.

"Why?" wondered the stranger.

"A return ticket is good only for three days and this one, as far as I can judge, was issued a year and a day ago. This ticket, my dear fellow, is no good."

"Damn it," said the stranger. "I hadn't thought of that! Now I'll have to buy another ticket and I haven't a penny left." He mused. "Wait a moment! Just as I ran off after my hat, I asked a man to hold my briefcase which held all my money."

"How much money was in that case?" asked the judge quickly.

"If I am not mistaken, there was one million three hundred sixty-seven thousand eight hundred fifteen crowns, ninety-two hellers, and a toothbrush."

"Precisely, to the dot," said the judge. "Here it is. The case, the money, the toothbrush and all. And there stands the man you asked to hold your case. His name is Francis King, and here Mr. Boura and I have just sentenced him to death for having robbed and murdered you."

"Well, what do you know!" exclaimed the stranger. "You say you locked him up? Well, at least he couldn't spend all the dough in the case."

The judge rose and solemnly proclaimed, "Now I know that Frank King did not steal, purloin, pilfer, filch, or snatch, nor did he make off with a single penny, nickel, dime, or quarter of the money deposited with him although he himself, as previously ascertained, didn't have even a penny to buy a roll or a small loaf of bread or other eatables or edibles called also bakery products or cereals, cerealia, in Latin. Hereby, let it be known that the said Francis King is declared innocent of murder, manslaughter, homicide, killing, burying of a corpse, robbery, violence, and thievery. Let it also be known that he waited day and night on the very spot, with honest intent, to return to the legal owner in full one million three hundred sixty-seven thousand eight hundred fifteen crowns and ninety-two hellers, and a toothbrush. I hereby declare him free of all charges, amen. Boy, was that a long speech!"

"I'll say!" said the stranger. "Let the honest tramp answer for himself."

"What should I say," asked Frank modestly. "I have never in my whole life taken anything from anybody. That's just how I am, I guess."

"You know you're a rare bird, not only among tramps but the rest of us, as well. A white crow, if there ever was one," the stranger pronounced.

"I'll second that!" added Boura the cop who, as you may have noticed, hadn't made a peep until now.

That's how Frank King was set free again. As a reward for his honesty, the stranger gave him enough money to buy himself a house; and into that house put a table; and on that table a plate; and on that plate a hot sausage. As it happened, Frank had a hole in his pocket, lost the money and again was left with nothing. He wandered where his legs carried him, all the way whistling on the whittle, but he couldn't get the white crow off his mind.

He spent that night in a shed and slept like a log. In the morning, when he peeked out, the sun was shining, the whole world glittered with fresh dew and on the fence, in front of the shed, sat a white crow. Frank, who had never before seen a white crow, stared at it, awestruck and breathless. The crow was as white as the freshly fallen snow, its eyes shone like rubies, its legs were the color of a rose and with its beak it was preening its feathers. When the crow caught a glimpse of Frank, it fluttered its wings, as if ready to fly off, but it stayed put, mistrustfully eyeing Frank's hairy head with one of its ruby eyes.

"You there," the crow uttered unexpectedly, "are you going to throw a stone at me?"

"No," answered Frank, and only then flinched at hearing the crow speak. "How can you talk?"

"It's not a big deal," said the crow. "All of us white crows can speak. Black crows can only caw, but I can say anything I like."

"You must be kidding," Frank said, amazed. "Well, say craw."

"Craw," said the crow.

"Now say crown," Frank asked.

"Crown," repeated the crow. "You see, I can talk. We white crows aren't just ordinary folk. True, a common crow knows how to count to five. But we white crows can count to seven. Look, one, two, three, four, five, six, seven. How about you?"

"At least to ten," said Frank.

"Now c'mon, let me hear you!"

"Ten and nine, soup would be just fine; nine, ten, for all hungry men."

"My word!" exclaimed the white crow, "you are one smart bird! We white crows are the cream of the bird crop. Haven't you noticed that people paint big birds with white goose wings and human beaks on the walls in their churches?"

"Hmmm," said Frank, "you mean angels."

"All right, angels," said the white crow. "They really are white crows, you know. You see, only a very few people have ever seen a white crow, as there are very few of us around."

"To be honest, I must tell you," said Frank, "they say I, too, am a white crow."

"Is that so," said the white crow doubtfully. "You aren't very white. Now who told you that?"

"Just yesterday, Mr. Šulc, the court magistrate, said so, and a stranger said it too, and so did Mr. Boura the policeman."

"I'll be . . ." The white crow was baffled. "Wait, who are you really?"

"My name's King, Frank King," said the tramp shyly.

"A king? You are a king?" exclaimed the crow. "You must be lying through your teeth. No king is this shabby."

"Well, I happen to be a shabby king."

"And in which country are you king?" asked the crow.

"Everywhere, I guess. Here, and when I'm in Skalica there, too, I'm King. The same in Trutnov—"

"How about in England?"

"In England, I'd be King too."

"But not in France."

"In France too. I'm Frank King no matter where I am."

"That's impossible!" said the crow. "Repeat after me: I cross my heart and hope to die."

"I cross my heart and hope to die," Frank swore.

"God is my witness."

"God is my witness," said Frank. "Let the earth open under me, if it's not the truth. May he strike me mute."

"That's enough," interrupted the crow. "And would you dare to be king among the white crows too?"

"Sure, even among white crows I would still be Frank King," he said.

"Then listen," said the white crow. "Today, over there, on Crow Mountain, we white crows hold an assembly to elect the king of all the crows. The king of all the crows is always a white crow. Now since you are a white crow, and a real king to boot, it's just possible you may get elected. Look, why don't you wait here until noon, then I'll be back with the election results."

"Fine, I'll wait," said Frank King. Then, the white crow spread its dazzling white wings and flew off to Crow Mountain, while Frank waited, basking in the sun.

You know, children, at election time there is always plenty of talking. Thus it happened that the crows on Crow Mountain quarreled and squabbled and hadn't been able to reach an agreement by the noon chime. It was only then that they began their roll call and finally did elect Frank King ruler of all crows.

In the meantime, Frank King became weary of waiting, and hungry as well, so after twelve o'clock he set

out for Hronov to my grandfather the miller for a taste of a crusty oven-fresh loaf of bread. So when the white crow returned with the news that Frank had been elected king, he was long gone, over the hills and dales.

The crows bewailed the loss of their king, and the white crows implored the black ones to fly all over the world to search for him, to summon him, and to bring him back to the crows' throne, in the forest of Crow Mountain.

Since that time crows have been flying all over the world, cawing ceaselessly. This is especially true in winter, when a bevy of them flock together. They burst from the ground, lifting off in unison, hovering over the fields and woods and cawing—in search of their king.

The
Great
Police
Tale

C hildren, I am sure you know that at every police station there are always a few policemen on duty all night long. Just in case of a burglary, or, if some hoodlums harm someone, the policemen are ready to help. That's why policemen are up and about the station until dawn while others, the so-called patrolmen, walk the streets and watch out for robbers, thieves, monsters, and other such mischief-makers. When their feet start aching they return to the station, and their replacements take over. That's how it goes the whole night through. At the station, to make the time pass, the policemen smoke pipes and tell each other about the curious things they have encountered.

Once, as they were all puffing and talking, a policeman returned from his patrol duty. Why, wasn't it Officer Halaburd? Yes, it was Halaburd all right, and he said, "Hey, guys! My feet are killing me, I humbly report."

"Then sit down!" said the senior officer. "Officer Holas will switch with you. So, tell us what's new on your beat, and what about the cases in which you had to intervene in the name of the law?"

"Nothing much happened tonight," said Officer Halaburd. "All I can remember were the two cats fighting on Štěpánská Street. In the name of the law I sent them packing after I reprimanded them. Then in Žitná Street a young sparrow residing at number twenty-three fell out of his nest. So, I called up the Old Town firemen, and asked them to come over with a ladder and return the sparrow to its nest. His parents were warned to keep an eye on him. As I stepped down Ječná Street, something yanked at my trouser. I looked down and saw an elf. You know, the one from Charles Square."

"Which one?" inquired the senior officer. "There are quite a few of them living there: Bubblewhiskers; Kobold, also known as Gramps; Banshee; Puck; Pumperlinck; Quackey, also known as Pipe; Chickfoot; and Tinto, who moved here from Appolinaire."

"It was Puck, the one who lives in the old willow. He pulled my trousers," said Officer Halaburd.

"Now that one is really nice," said the senior officer. "Any time someone loses anything in the park around here, let's say a ring, a ball, a top, or a rattle, Puck always brings it to one of the guards. An honest fellow, that Puck. Continue."

"All right, so this Puck is telling me," continued Officer Halaburd, 'Officer, I can't go home to my place in the old willow because a squirrel crawled in and she won't budge.' So, I drew my saber, followed Puck to his willow, and ordered that squirrel, in the name of the law, to vacate the premises. Also, I issued a warning not to trespass, not to commit crimes, misdemeanors and obstructions, such as illegal tenancy, disturbing the peace, violence and larceny. The squirrel snapped, 'I'll leave when hell freezes over, and not before!' So I took off my cloak and belt and climbed the willow. When I reached the hollow in a gnarled branch where Mr. Puck has his stall, the squirrel started to wail, 'Officer, please, don't arrest me! I holed up here at Mr. Puck's because it rained, and my place is flooded!' 'Stop yakking,' I said to her, 'pack your stuff, get your beechnuts, and get off Mr. Puck's property! If you enter Mr. Puck's private quarters ever again without his consent, or his go-ahead, we'll call reinforcements, surround you, arrest you, and haul you handcuffed to the police station. Now, shoo!' That's all I've seen tonight."

"I must say, I've never seen an elf," said Officer Bambas. "In those new buildings in Dejvice, where I've been stationed until now, you won't find any phantoms, bogeys, or supernatural phenomena, as they are called today."

"We've got oodles of them here," said the senior officer. "And in the old days, good Lord, there were millions of them. Since the beginning of time, there used to be a water sprite living in the Fidgety Weir. Police never had anything to do with him, for he was an honest fellow. That water sprite from Liběň may have been an old rascal, but

the one from Fidgety Weir was an upright citizen. Did you
know that the Prague Sanitary District named him Chief
City Water Sprite and put him on the payroll? It was his
job to make sure that the river Moldau didn't dry out. He
never caused any floods, though, like the water sprites
from the country. Now, the Liben water sprite egged on
the one from Fidgety Weir to demand that he be named
municipal counsel of the City of Prague, and be paid ac-
cordingly. He did just that! When City Hall told him it was
impossible because he lacked the required academic cre-
dentials, he was so upset he moved out of Prague. Now
he's making waves in Dresden, or so they say. It's common

knowledge that every water sprite on the Elbe river in Germany, all the way to the city of Hamburg, is a staunch Czech. Well then, ever since he moved, there hasn't been another water sprite in Fidgety Weir, and there hasn't been enough water in Prague either!

"Also, in Charles Square, there were will-o'-the-wisps, dancing all night long. Since they were a nuisance, and people were afraid of them, the Prague City Council made a deal: they would move to City Park, and there they would be lit at night and put out at dawn by an employee of the gasworks. But since that man enlisted during the war, the will-o'-the-wisps have been left to fend for themselves.

"On the subject of fairies, in City Park alone there used to be seventeen, but three joined a ballet theater, one became a film star, and another got married to a railroad engineer from Střešovice. So now there are three fairies in Kinský Gardens, two up around Gröb Street, and another in Deer Trench. The park attendant of Rieger Park intended to house one of them there, but she somehow didn't take to it; the place must have been too drafty for her. In Prague, there are three hundred and forty-six elves registered with the police, residing in public buildings, parks, convents, and libraries. That's without counting those imps who live in private homes and who can't be documented.—And think of ghosts! Prague had them galore, but when it was scientifically proven that ghosts didn't exist, they were abolished. Rumor has it that people in the Lesser Quarter still harbor a handful of timeworn spooks in their attics; at least that's what a colleague of mine from the local headquarters told me the other day. Well, as far as I know, that's it."

"To say nothing of that dragon," said Officer Kubát, "you know, the monster they killed in the limekilns at Žižkov!"

"I wouldn't know much about that monster, Žižkov was never on my beat."

"I was there when it happened," said Officer Kubát, "but the case was handled by Officer Vokoun. It was a very long time ago. The late Mr. Bienert was the police commissioner then. Well, it all started one evening with an old lady named Mrs. Cástek. She was the tobacconist, but let me tell you, she was really a psychic or sooth-sayer, or something like that. So Mrs. Částek told Officer Vokoun that she had read in her cards that Huldabord the monster had kidnapped a beautiful maiden from her parents and was keeping her prisoner in the limekilns at Žižkov. The maiden was the Murcian princess, according to Mrs. Částek.

" 'Murcian or not Murcian, the monster must return the girl to her parents,' Vokoun said, 'or I'll begin proceedings against him according to regulations titled Service Order, Rules, or Instructions.' Having said that, he donned his belt and sword, and so equipped, he went to the limekilns. I have no doubt that we all would have done the same."

"No doubt about it," said Officer Bambas, "but I've never had a dragon in Dejvice or Střešovice, so continue!"

"Well then, Officer Vokoun fastened his belt and holster, and in the middle of the night, he left for Žižkov. There from a dark hole he heard a clamor of harsh voices. When he flicked on his bull's eye lantern, he caught sight of a ghoulish, seven-headed monster. All the monster's heads talked to each other, answered one another, squabbled, and insulted each other. Well, you can certainly imagine that such a monster wouldn't have manners, and if he had any, he would have only bad ones. And there she was, a beautiful maiden right there with the monster. She was crying bitterly and plugging her ears as to shut out the awful voices of the monster's heads.

" 'Hello there,' Officer Vokoun called out to the monster, politely to be sure, but with official gravity,

'mind showing me your papers? Do you have an ID? A gun permit? A library card? Voter's registration? Anything?'

"One of the monster's heads jeered, one blasphemed, another cursed, one swore, another called names, one made fun of him, and still another stuck its tongue out at him. Officer Vokoun wouldn't give in, and exclaimed, 'In the name of the law, get moving, and follow me to headquarters! You, and that girl behind you, too!'

" 'Keep your trap shut!' shrieked one of the heads. 'Don't you know who I am, you human featherweight? I am Huldabord the dragon!'

"'Huldabord from Granada mountains,' cried the second head.

"'Also known as the Great Dragon from Mulhouse,' yelled the third head.

"'And I'll gobble you up like a raspberry,' roared the fourth.

"'I'll burst you to snippets, I'll shred you to smithereens, I'll hash you and squash you, I'll slice you in half like a pickled herring, and I'll shake sawdust out of you!' thundered the fifth head.

"'I'll wring your neck!' boomed the sixth.

"'And then, you little twit, you can whistle your death song,' chimed in the seventh head in a terrible voice.

"Now tell me, what do you think Officer Vokoun did then? Do you think that maybe he got the jitters? C'mon fellows! When he realized he wouldn't get anywhere by being polite, he got out his club, and with all his might he began whacking the dragon's heads, one after another, and he was no lightweight!

"'Now look at that!' said the first head. 'Not bad at all!'

"'Something just grazed my forehead,' said the second.

"'A flea just bit my neck,' remarked the third.

"'Darling,' said the fourth head, 'would you mind striking me again with that little twig?'

"'But try harder,' suggested the fifth, 'so it crackles a little!'

"'More to the left,' demanded the sixth, 'that's where it itches dreadfully.'

" 'That little softie of yours is too flimsy for me,'
taunted the seventh. 'Don't you have anything stronger?'

"At that point Officer Vokoun drew his sword
and slashed each head once till their scales rattled.

" 'Getting a bit better,' said the first head.

" 'You did lop off a flea's ear, at any rate,'
grinned the second. 'My fleas are made of steel, you see.'

" 'And you clipped that one hair that itched,'
said the third.

" 'Raked my coiffure,' the fourth head said with
delight.

" 'I wouldn't mind if you scratched me every day
with that little rake,' growled the fifth.

" 'I couldn't even feel that feather,' the sixth complained.

" 'Hey, buddy,' said the seventh, 'tickle me again, would you?'

"Officer Vokoun grabbed his revolver and pumped seven shots, one into each of the dragon's heads.

" 'Oh my god!' shrieked the monster, 'stop throwing sand at me! It will get into my hair! Holy smoke! A speck just got into my eye! And another got stuck between my teeth! Now I've just about had it! The show's over!' The dragon roared, cleared his seven throats, and spewed flames at Officer Vokoun from all his seven jaws. Officer Vokoun, unfazed, pulled out his manual of service regulations and thumbed through it to determine what a policeman should do when up against overwhelming odds. Yes, there it was—in such a case he should call for reinforcements. Then he looked up the guidelines for action during a blaze, and he was instructed to call the fire department. Having carefully reviewed all the instructions, he called the firemen and requested police reinforcements. Six of us, Officers Rabas, Holas, Matlas, Kudlas, Firbas, and myself, arrived trotting, and Officer Vokoun told us, 'Look fellows, we've got to free the girl from the brute force of that dragon. It's true that this dragon is made of steel, and it's also true that for a dragon like him any sword is too weak. But I've taken a careful look and I've discovered his soft spot. When I count to three, all of you slash him right in the nape of his neck, but first, the fire-fighters have to put him out so he doesn't burn our uniforms.' He had barely finished when up drove seven

fire engines with seven firemen each. 'Firemen to attention!' shouted Officer Vokoun bravely. 'When I count to
three, each of you will jet water on one of the dragon's
heads, aiming directly at the throat, because he shoots the
flames directly from his tonsils. Get ready: one-two-three!'
As he said 'three' the firemen aimed seven jet streams into
the dragon's jaws where the fire blazed. S-s-s-s, it hissed,
let me tell you! The dragon spat and hawked, spewed and
slobbered, frothed and coughed, sputtered and spluttered,
rattled and roared, panted and swore, called 'mommy!' and
thrashed his tail around, but the firemen didn't let up.
They kept on squirting and spurting until, instead of a

flickering flame, steam gushed out of the dragon's gullets, and you couldn't see two steps ahead of you. When the steam thinned out, the firemen stopped squirting, blew their horns, and went home. And the dragon, drenched and quite shriveled, just sputtered and spat and wiped water from his eyes, snarling, 'Just you wait, you scoundrels, I'll get even with you!' But Officer Vokoun was already shouting, 'Get ready—one-two-three!' At the sound of 'three' we swung our sabers and slashed the dragon's seven napes, and his seven heads rolled. Out of his seven necks gushed all the water from the fire engines, spraying like an open hydrant. 'Let's go now,' said Officer Vokoun to the Murcian princess, 'but be careful not to splatter your lovely dress.'

" 'Thanks a million, gallant hero,' said the maiden, 'for setting me free from that monster's clutches. I was playing ball, and catch, and hide-and-seek with my friends in the park when that fat old dragon flew in, kidnapped me, and carried me off, non-stop, to this place.'

" 'And what route did you take, young lady?' inquired Officer Vokoun.

" 'Across Algiers, over Malta, Constantinople, Belgrade, Vienna, Znojmo, Čáslav, Záběhlice, Strašnice, to here in thirty-two hours, seven minutes, and five seconds, non-stop, full stop,' said the Murcian princess.

" 'That's a record time for a passenger flight,' said Officer Vokoun in amazement. 'Congratulations, Miss. And now I'd better send out a cable to your esteemed father and ask him to send someone to fetch you.'

"He had barely finished speaking when a car roared up. The Murcian king, dressed in ermine and brocade, sprang out and began jumping with joy on one leg, while cheering, 'Sweetheart, I've found you at last!'

" 'Wait a moment, Your Highness,' Officer Vokoun cut him short. 'With that car of yours, you have exceeded the legal speed limit. I have to write you a ticket. The fine's seven crowns.'

"The Murcian king began to rummage in his pockets, and complained, 'Have I lost my mind? I know I brought with me seven hundred doubloons, piasters, and ducats, one thousand pesetas, three thousand six hundred francs, eight hundred and twenty marks, one thousand two hundred and sixteen Czechoslovak crowns and ninety-five hellers, and now I'm flat broke. Most likely I've spent it all on gas and speeding tickets. Brave knight, I shall have my assistant forward those seven crowns to you.' Whereupon the Murcian king cleared his throat, placed his hand to his breast, and continued, 'Your uniform and your noble countenance suggest a mighty warrior, prince, or perhaps even a civil servant, and since you have slain the ghoulish Mulhouse dragon and set my daughter free, I should offer you her hand. I see however that you have a wedding band on your finger, whereby I presume that you are already taken. Any children?'

" 'Yes,' Vokoun said, 'a boy of three, and a baby girl.'

" 'Congratulations,' said the Murcian king. 'All I have is this one daughter. But wait! Why don't I give you half of my Murcian kingdom? In rough estimates that's seventy thousand four hundred fifty-nine square miles of ground, with seven thousand one hundred and five miles of railroads, twelve thousand miles of roads, and twenty-

two million seven hundred and fifty thousand nine hundred and eleven subjects of both sexes. Is it a deal?'

" 'Your Majesty, I have a hunch that there may be a slight hitch,' reckoned Officer Vokoun. 'My colleagues and I killed that dragon in the course of official duty because he wouldn't obey my summons and accompany me to headquarters. For carrying out one's duty one mustn't accept any reward whatsoever! Good Lord! That's totally prohibited!'

" 'Now what if I made the offer of half of the Murcian kingdom with all the appurtenances as a token of my gratitude to the Prague Police Department? How would that go over?'

" 'That sounds more likely,' suggested Officer Vokoun. 'But that too could turn out to be a fine kettle of fish. Look, we already have to be at the beck and call of the whole Prague district. You wouldn't believe all the walking and surveillance that requires! Now if you added half of the Murcian kingdom to it, we'd have to traipse too far, and our feet would ache. We really are much obliged, Your Majesty, but Prague is big enough already.'

" 'Well then,' said the Murcian king, 'why don't I at least give you officers a tobacco pouch that I brought with me on my journey. It's genuine Murcian tobacco, and it will just do for seven pipes if you stuff them full. Now, darling,' he addressed his daughter, 'hop into the car, and off we go!'

"When he had disappeared in a cloud of dust—and he made a colossal cloud of dust—we, that is to say, Officers Rabas, Holas, Matlas, Kudlas, Firbas, Vokoun, and myself, went to the Police Station and stuffed our pipes with that genuine Murcian tobacco. Let me tell you, fellows, such tobacco I have never smoked in my entire life! It wasn't too pungent, but it smelled like honey, like vanilla, like tea, like cinnamon, like incense, like carnations and like bananas. But as our pipes gave off a vintage stench, the flavor of the Murcian tobacco was totally lost on us. The dragon should have been put in a museum, but before they could get him there, he turned into aspic since he was thoroughly soaked, and had gone sour. And that's all I have to report."

* * *

Officer Kubát had concluded his tale of the Žižkov monster, and his fellow policemen went on puffing in silence, thinking no doubt of that Murcian tobacco. Then Officer Choděra spoke. "Now that Officer Kubát has told you of the Žižkov dragon, let me tell you about the hydra from Vojtěsská Street. Once, as I was walking along Vojtěsská on my beat, I spotted an enormous egg right there in one of the church nooks. The egg was so huge it wouldn't have fit into my service helmet, and it was as heavy as marble. Whew! Is this an ostrich egg or what, I said to myself. I'll take it to the Lost and Found at the station. Who knows, its owner may claim it. At that time, Officer Pour was in charge of Lost and Found. He just happened to have caught a cold, and his back ached. So, to soothe himself, he had a fire going in the iron stove. You wouldn't have believed the heat! The place was as hot as an oven, what am I saying, like a furnace, why, like a brick kiln.

" 'Pour, man,' I said, 'it's as warm here as at the devil's grandmother's! I report that I found an egg in Vojtěšská Street.'

" 'Then put it somewhere,' said Pour, 'and sit down. Let me tell you about this pain in my back, what a pest it has been.'

"Well, one word led to another, and I'd say we chatted till nightfall. Suddenly, something crackled and rustled in the corner. When we turned the light on, we gasped. Would you believe it? A hydra had hatched out of that egg! The extreme heat must have made it hatch. It wasn't much larger than a poodle or, perhaps, a fox terrier, but there was no doubt that it was a hydra. That we recognized at once, for it had seven heads, and you can always tell a hydra by its heads.

" 'Good Lord!' cried Pour, 'what will we do with it here? I'd better call the scavengers, they'll get rid of it!'

" 'Pour,' I said, 'before you call, you ought to know that a hydra like this is a very rare animal. What we should really do is to place an ad in the paper for the owner to come forth.'

" 'Sure, why not,' said Pour, 'but in the meantime, what will we feed it? All right, I'll try milk and breadcrumbs. Milk is the healthiest food for any tyke.'

"So he crumbled up seven dinner rolls into seven pints of milk, and you should have seen how ravenously that tiny hydra went for it! One head pushed the other

away from the saucer, all the heads growled at each other
and lapped up the milk until they messed up the whole
room. Then one head after the other smacked its lips and
dozed off, whereupon Officer Pour locked it up in the office, together with all the lost and found articles from all of
Prague, and placed the following ad in the paper:

F O U N D

H Y D R A P U P P Y

freshly hatched from the egg. Seven-headed, yellow, tiger-striped. Call or claim it in person at Police Headquarters, Lost and Found Department.

"Next morning, when Officer Pour arrived at his office, he gave out a scream: 'Holy Moses! For crying out loud! Holy cow! Holy smoke! Holy mackerel! Cheese and crackers! I'll be . . . !' During the night, the hydra had gobbled up every single thing that anybody had lost or found in the city of Prague: rings and watches, wallets and purses, bags and notebooks, balls and pencils, penholders and pens, textbooks and marbles, buttons and rulers, gloves, and all the official papers and documents, records and certificates, and even Pour's pipe, coal shovel, and the ruler that the good officer used for lining his papers. The hydra had gorged on so much of the stuff that it was already twice as large as the day before, and some of its heads were nauseous from overeating.

" 'This can't go on,' said Officer Pour, 'I can't keep this beast here.' So he called the Anti-Cruelty Society and requested that the reputable body provide a shelter for the hydra puppy, as it would for stray dog puppies and kittens. 'Sure,' said the Society, and took the hydra puppy into its shelter. 'But we would like to know what to feed it. There's no reference to a hydra in science textbooks.' So they fed it milk, hot dogs, sausage, eggs, carrots, porridge, chocolate, black pudding, green peas, hay, soup, grain, headcheese, tomatoes, rice, rolls, sugar, potatoes, and mag-

gots, and the hydra gobbled it all up and, on top of that, devoured all their books, newspapers, paintings, and door-knobs. In short, it ate up everything the Society owned and grew bigger than a Saint Bernard.

"Then, the Society's office received a cable from faraway Bucharest, written in magic script:

> *Hydra Pup is a Spellbound Human* **STOP** *Further*
> *Details in Person* **STOP** *Will Arrive at Wilson RR*
> *Station in Three Hundred Years* **STOP**
> *Bosco the Magician*

"The Society director scratched his ear, and said, 'For heavens' sake! If that hydra is a person under a spell, then it's a human, and we can't keep it in an animal shelter. We'll have to transfer it to a shelter for the homeless or to an orphanage.' But all the shelters for the homeless and all the orphanages said, 'Whew! If this person has been changed into an animal, it's no longer a human being, but an animal, for it's been changed into one. A person under a spell doesn't enter under our jurisdiction but belongs to the Anti-Cruelty Society.' Since they couldn't reach an agreement as to whether a human transformed into an animal was more of a human or an animal, neither one nor the other wanted to keep the hydra, and the poor thing didn't know to whom it actually belonged. That made the hydra so miserable that it stopped eating, especially the third, fifth, and seventh heads.

"Now, working at the Anti-Cruelty Society was a short, slender little man, inconspicuous and modest as an empty shell. His name began with the letter N: something like Naught, Nihil, Nulty—no, actually his name was Trutina. And when Mr. Trutina saw one hydra head after another wilt with grief, he told the Society, 'Gentlemen, I don't care if it is a human or an animal. I'd like to take the hydra home with me, and I'll take care of it properly.' And they all said, 'Hallelujah!' and Mr. Trutina took the hydra home.

"You'd have to admit that Mr. Trutina took care of the beast admirably: he fed it, combed its hair, and patted it—you see, Mr. Trutina was very fond of animals—and every evening after he came home from work he took it out for a walk to get some fresh air. The hydra romped around like a puppy, wriggled its tail, and answered to the name Amina. One evening, a dogcatcher saw them and in-

quired: 'Now look at this! What sort of an animal have you got here, Mr. Trutina? If it's a beast of prey, a rapacious vulture, a savage brute, well, you mustn't walk it on the streets! And if it's a dog, you must buy a tag for its collar.'

" 'Amina is a rare breed of dog,' said Mr. Trutina, 'the so-called dragon terrier or dracobeagle, the seven-headed retriever. Isn't it so, Amina? Don't you worry, I'll buy her a tag.' The poor fellow bought a dog tag although he had to shell out his last coin. Again, the dogcatcher saw them, and said: 'Oh no, Mr. Trutina, this won't work! If that pup of yours has seven heads, it must have seven tags! For the regulation says that every dog must have a tag on its neck.'

" 'But sir,' implored Mr. Trutina, 'Amina has a tag on her middle neck!'

" 'Makes no difference!' said the dogcatcher. 'Still, she's got six heads running about without tags, and that I won't tolerate! I'll have to seize that cur!'

" 'I beg you sir, please wait three more days, won't you? I'll buy the tags for Amina.' And he walked home crestfallen, for he hadn't a single penny left.

"At home, he sat down and very nearly cried, for he felt so rueful thinking about the dogcatcher taking Amina away from him, and selling her to a circus or putting her to sleep. As he agonized and moaned, the hydra drew close to him, lay all her seven heads in his lap, and gazed at him with such sad and beautiful eyes, eyes so handsome and nearly human that all animals have when they look at a person with love and trust.

" 'I won't let them take you away, Amina,' said Mr. Trutina and stroked her seven heads. Then he took the watch his late father had left to him, his Sunday suit, and his best pair of shoes, sold them all, and borrowed some money as well, and for all that money he bought six dog tags and hung them on the hydra's collars. And when he took her out to the street, all the tags jingled and tinkled just as if a sleigh with bells were passing.

"The very same evening, his landlord came to him, and said, 'Mr. Trutina, I don't seem able to take to that dog of yours. Granted, I'm no expert in dogs, but there

are rumors that it's a hydra. If that's so, I can't have it in my house.'

" 'But sir,' said Mr. Trutina, 'Amina hasn't harmed anyone!'

" 'I don't give a hoot!' said the landlord, 'a respectable building won't tolerate a hydra on its premises, and that's it! If you don't get rid of that animal, you're out of here on the first of next month. Have a good evening, Mr. Trutina.' And he slammed the door behind him.

" 'See, Amina, to top it off, we'll have to move,' wept Mr. Trutina. 'But I won't let you go.' Shuffling her paws very softy, the hydra drew close to him, and her eyes shone with such exceptional beauty that Mr. Trutina could barely stand it. 'Well, well, old girl,' he said, 'I'm fond of you, you know.'

"Full of worries, he went to work the following day. (He was a bank clerk.) Once there, the manager called him in. 'Mr. Trutina,' said the manager, 'it's true that your private affairs are none of my business, but having said that, let me tell you that strange rumors are circulating about your keeping some sort of hydra at home. Look, none of your superiors keep a hydra. Only a king or maybe a sultan can afford one. Hydras are not pets for ordinary folks. You, Mr. Trutina, seem to live well above your means. Now, you either get rid of that beast or you are fired.'

" 'Sir,' Mr. Trutina said softly but resolutely, 'I will not forsake Amina!' And he walked home feeling a grief impossible to fathom.

"At home he sat down as if his were a body bereft of its soul, and tears began to fill his eyes. 'This is the end of me,' he said to himself, and wept. He felt one of the hydra's heads in his lap. He couldn't see her through his tears, but he stroked her and murmured, 'Don't worry, Amina, I won't let you go.' And as he kept stroking the head, it seemed to become softer and curlier. He wiped the tears from his eyes and looked. There, before him, instead of a hydra, knelt a lovely maiden, leaning with her chin against his knees, and gazing sweetly into his eyes.

" 'Good Lord!' cried Mr. Trutina. 'Where is Amina?'

" 'I am Princess Amina,' said the maiden. 'Until this very moment I was under a spell, as a hydra, for I was proud and petulant, but from now on, Mr. Trutina, I'll be as good and sweet as a lamb.'

" 'Amen,' said a voice in the door. Lo, there stood Bosco the magician. 'You have redeemed her, Mr. Trutina. You see, love liberates humans and animals from their magic spells. [Now tell me, children, isn't that a good ending!] As for you, Mr. Trutina, I have a message for you from this young lady's father. You are to come to his kingdom and ascend to the throne. Now let's go, so we don't miss the train!'

"And that's the end of 'The Case of the Hydra,' added Officer Choděra. If you have any doubts about what I've just told you, check it out with Officer Pour."

*The
Mailman's
Tale*

C an you tell me why, if there are fairy tales about people in all kinds of professions—about kings, princes, robbers, shepherds, knights, magicians, giants, lumberjacks, and water sprites—couldn't there be a fairy tale about a mailman? After all, the post office looks almost like an enchanted place, with all those signs like No Smoking!, No Dogs!, and plenty of other bills and warning notices. Believe me, not even magicians or dragons have so many public notices and prohibitions on display in their chambers. That clearly implies that a post office is a mysterious and formidable place. Children, have any of you ever seen what happens in a post office after hours when it's closed? Probably not. Then why don't we peek in? A mailman by the name of Mr. Kolbaba has seen it all with his own eyes, and he has told the rest of the letter carriers and mailmen and they have passed it on, and that's how I heard about it. I am not so selfish that I would keep it to myself, so let's begin.

Mr. Kolbaba, the letter carrier and mailman, grew weary of his job. He complained that day in and day out a mailman had to walk, rush, plod, dash and trudge so much. He claimed to walk twenty-nine thousand seven hundred thirty-five steps, and that included eight thousand two hundred forty-nine steps upstairs and downstairs. And he was also overheard to say that the letters he carried contained, at best, printed matter, bills, and other useless stuff that didn't make anyone very happy, and that the post office itself was such a dreary, good-for-nothing place about which no fairy tales could be written. Mr. Kolbaba bemoaned his mailman's job in many ways. Then one day out of sheer dejection he sat down by the stove in the post office and fell asleep, without even noticing it was

almost six o'clock. At six all the mailmen and letter carriers left, closing the post office behind them, leaving Mr. Kolbaba locked in and asleep.

It must have been around midnight when a noise that sounded as if mice were tapping on the floor awoke him. "What do you know, we've got mice here!" thought Mr. Kolbaba to himself. "Someone should set a trap for them." He went looking for the mice but soon found out that they weren't mice at all, only postal elves. Postal elves are tiny bearded minikins, just about as big as a smallish Wyandotte hen, or a squirrel, or a wild rabbit—well, just about as big as that. They wear mailmen caps like real mailmen and capes like real letter carriers. "Well, I'll be . . ." said Mr. Kolbaba to himself, but otherwise he didn't utter a sound, not a word, not even a peep, for fear of frightening them away. Now would you believe that one of the elves was rearranging the letters that Mr. Kolbaba was to deliver next day? Another was sorting the mail, and a third was weighing the parcels and sticking labels on them. The fourth elf muttered about a box that wasn't tied up according to postal regulations; the fifth sat at the window tallying the money, just like postal employees usually do. "I knew it," mumbled the elf, "the clerk made a mistake, and now it's up to me to fix it." A sixth imp sat at the telegraph machine tapping out a message that sounded like: tactac tac tac tactac tac. Mr. Kolbaba understood the message which, in ordinary language, read: hello there p.o. headquarters postal imp number one hundred thirty-one reporting that all is well stop elf doublebeard has cold reported sick stop not on duty stop.

"Here's a letter addressed to the city of Bambo-limbonanda in the Cannibal Kingdom," uttered the seventh elf. "Where is that?"

"That's via Benešov," said the eighth minikin. "Why don't you write on it Cannibal Kingdom, Lower Trebizon, near Kitty Castle. By air. That's enough. Now how about a game of cards, gentlemen?"

"Why not," said the first elf, and counted out thirty-two letters. "Here are the cards, let's start."

The second whippersnapper took the letters and shuffled them.

"I'll cut," said the first imp.

"Someone deal!" said the second.

"I've got a bad hand," muttered the third one.

"I'll open," said the fourth, and slapped a letter on the table.

"I can beat that," said the fifth, and put his letter on top.

"That's too easy, my boy," said the sixth, and played his letter.

"Uh-huh," said the seventh, "I've got a better one."

"And here's an ace," called out the eighth, and played his trump card.

At that point, Mr. Kolbaba couldn't stand it any longer, and blurted out, "Don't let me interrupt you, gentlemen, but may I ask what cards you've got there?"

"Ah, Mr. Kolbaba," said the first elf. "We didn't want to wake you, but now that you are up anyway, why not come and join us in a game. We are playing a simple game of whist."

Mr. Kolbaba didn't need to be asked again and joined the elves.

"Here's your hand," the second elf told him, and passed him some letters. "Go ahead."

Mr. Kolbaba looked at the letters and said, "I hope you won't mind if I point out to you, gentlemen, that the only cards I've got are undelivered letters."

"That's right," said the third minikin, "those are our playing cards."

"Hum," Mr. Kolbaba went on, "no offense, gentlemen, but playing cards begin at seven, then comes eight, nine, ten, jack, queen, and king, with ace being the highest. But here, in these letters there's nothing of that sort."

"You are greatly mistaken, Mr. Kolbaba," the fourth tiny man told him, "just so you know, every letter counts for whatever is written in it."

"The lowest cards, or sevens, are those letters in which people tell lies and pretend to each other," explained the first elf.

"The second lowest card is eight," the second imp continued. "Those are the letters people write to each other because they have to; in other words, letters written out of obligation."

"The third lowest card is nine," the third imp went on. "Those are letters people write only out of politeness."

"The next is ten," said the fourth. "In those letters people write something interesting and new to each other."

"The next highest card is the jack," said the fifth, "and those are letters that people write to give pleasure to others."

"The third highest card is the queen," the sixth was saying. "Those are letters between good friends."

"The fourth highest card is king," added the seventh. "That's a letter written out of love."

"And the highest card, or ace," the eighth little old man chimed in, "is a letter in which a person puts his whole heart. That card beats or trumps all the rest. That could be a letter that a mother writes to her child, or any person, to someone he loves more than himself."

"Uh-huh," said Mr. Kolbaba. "But now I'd like to know how in the world you find out what's written in these letters because I would certainly hate to hear that you open and read them. You mustn't do that, gentlemen, that much you know. You'd be breaking the law of privacy, and I'd have to report it to the police. Holy smoke! Opening a letter that doesn't belong to you is a monstrous sin!"

"We know that too, Mr. Kolbaba," said the first elf. "We know the content of each letter simply by touch. Indifferent letters are cold to the touch. The more love the letter contains, the warmer it is."

"If we put a letter to our forehead," said the second, "we can tell what's in it word for word."

"Well, that's a completely different story," said Mr. Kolbaba. "Now that we are here together, I'd like to ask you something else, and please don't get offended."

"Well, since it's you, Mr. Kolbaba, ask anything you'd like," said the third minikin.

"I'd like to know what you elves eat," said Mr. Kolbaba.

"It depends," the fourth elf answered. "We elves who live in various offices feed like cockroaches on what-

ever you people drop: breadcrumbs, bits of cake—well, there isn't much that you people drop from your mouth."

"But we postal elves cannot complain. Sometimes, we cook telegraph tapes like noodles, then dab some glue on them, but the glue must have dextrin in it."

"We lick the stamps too," mentioned the sixth one. "The glue tastes delicious, except that it makes our beards too gooey."

"Mostly, though, we eat crumbs," explained the seventh manikin. "That's why offices aren't swept very often, you know, so there will be some crumbs left for us."

"Dare I ask where you sleep?" Mr. Kolbaba queried.

"That, we won't tell you, Mr. Kolbaba," said the eighth tiny old man. "If people knew where we imps live, they'd sweep us out. No, that you mustn't know."

"If you won't tell me, keep it to yourself," thought Mr. Kolbaba. "I'll watch you." Then he moved back to the stove and sat down to watch. No sooner did he snuggle in than his eyelids grew heavy, and before one could even count to five, Mr. Kolbaba dozed off and slept like a log until morning.

* * *

Now you should know that Mr. Kolbaba, the mailman, revealed nothing of what he had seen to anyone. How could he, when it was forbidden to spend a night in the post office? Since then, though, he has never minded delivering the mail. "This letter," he'd say to himself, "is barely tepid, but this one, on the other hand, is so warm, it almost warms me up, just like a letter a mother would have written."

One day at the post office, as he was sorting letters he had taken out of the mailbox for delivery, he suddenly exclaimed, "Look at that! A letter in a sealed envelope, without an address, and without postage either!"

"Aha," said the postmaster, "again someone dropped a letter into the mailbox and forgot to address it."

Just then, a gentleman happened to be mailing a registered letter to his mother. He overheard the postmaster's remark and said, "That must have been a fool, a silly-

billy, a noodle, an idiot, a good-for-nothing, a dumbbell, if
he mailed a letter and didn't address it to anyone."

"Oh no, sir," said the postmaster, "throughout
the year, a heap of them piles up. You wouldn't believe,
sir, how many people are absentminded. They write a letter, then rush in a mad dash to the post office, forgetting,
sir, to check if they have addressed it. Oh yes, that happens more often than you'd think, sir."

"You don't say," wondered the gentleman.
"What do you do then with those letters that have no address on them?"

"Well, since we have no way to deliver them, we keep them here, sir," said the postmaster.

While this exchange was going on, Mr. Kolbaba was turning over the letter without an address, mumbling to himself. "Sir," he muttered, "this letter is so warm, it no doubt contains something impassioned. Address or no address, I believe it ought to be delivered to the person to whom it belongs."

"Without an address it can't be delivered, and that's that," insisted the postmaster.

"You could open it, couldn't you," suggested the stranger, "to see who sent it."

"Can't be done, sir," the postmaster intoned sternly, "that would constitute breaking the law of privacy, no, that can't be done." As far as he was concerned, the matter was settled.

After the stranger had left, Mr. Kolbaba turned to the postmaster and said, "Sorry for being so bold, sir, but I propose that a postal elf help us with this letter." He told the story of how one night he had seen the postal elves at work and how they could read letters without opening them.

The postmaster did a bit of hard thinking, and then said, "Well, that may do. Let's give it a try, Mr. Kolbaba. If an elf tells us what's in this letter, we may find out to whom it belongs."

That night, Mr. Kolbaba let himself be locked in the post office, and waited. It must have been midnight when, again, tap-tap, he heard the sound of mice scuttling about. He saw the elves sorting letters, weighing parcels, tallying money, tapping out dispatches. And when they were through with everything, they squatted on the floor and played whist with the letters.

That's when Mr. Kolbaba broke the silence. "Evening, gentlemen."

"Ah, Mr. Kolbaba is here," said the eldest imp. "Come closer and have a game with us!"

Mr. Kolbaba didn't need to be asked twice, and he joined them on the floor.

"I'll open," said the first elf, and played his card on the floor.

"I pass," said the second.

"I'll beat that," the third was saying.

Now it was Mr. Kolbaba's turn, and he put the sealed letter without an address on top of the others.

"You have won, Mr. Kolbaba," said the first little imp, "yours was the highest card, ace of hearts."

"Excuse me for taking the liberty," said Mr. Kolbaba, "but are you sure that it's really an ace?"

"Of course I'm sure," answered the elf. "It's a letter a young lad has written to the girl he loves more than himself."

"It's just that it somehow doesn't seem right," said Mr. Kolbaba.

"But it is," insisted the dwarf. "Now if you don't believe me, let me read you what's in the letter." He took the letter, held it to his forehead, closed his eyes, and read:

" 'Marie, my dearest beloved,

" 'I rite ["That's misspelled," the elf said. "It should have a 'w' "] to you to say that I got the job as a driver so if you like why we mite tie the not so rite me

wether you love me stil and rite soon yours truely Frankie.' "

"Thank you, sir. Well, that's all I needed to know. Many thanks indeed."

"Don't mention it," said the little man. "There are eight spelling mistakes in it, if you're interested. That Frankie, whoever he may be, didn't learn much in school."

"Now all I have to find out is which Marie and which Frankie they are," muttered Mr. Kolbaba.

"Sorry, Mr. Kolbaba, with that I can't help you, it's not written here," said the tiny man.

The next morning, Mr. Kolbaba reported to the postmaster that the letter without an address had been written by Frankie, a driver, to Marie, a young lady, and that Frankie wanted to take this maiden for his wife.

"Dear Lord!" exclaimed the postmaster, "now I'd say that's an extremely important letter! That letter most definitely should get to the young lady!"

"I'd deliver it immediately, if I only knew Marie's last name, the town she lives in, the street and the number," said Mr. Kolbaba.

"Anybody could do that," said the postmaster. "And he need not be a mailman! I'd really like to see to it that the young lady gets the letter!"

"Very well, sir," uttered Mr. Kolbaba. "If it takes a year, if I need to cross the whole world, I'll search for her!"

Having said that, he slung the mailbag containing the letter and a chunk of bread over his shoulder, and set off on his search.

Mr. Kolbaba traipsed and tramped everywhere, asking for a Miss Marie who might be expecting a letter from Frankie, a driver. He traversed the country around Litoměřice and Louny, and the district of Rakovník, and around Pilsen, and Tábor, and the captainship of Hradec and Čáslav, he walked over the Jičín district, and over the Boleslav region; he passed through Kutná Hora, Litomyšl, Třeboň, Vodňany, Sušica, Příbram, Kladno, Mladá Boleslav, Votice, Trutnov, Sobotka, Turnov, Sláně and Pelhřimov. He even reached Dobruška, Úpice, Hronov, The Seven Cottages, Crow Mountain, and Zálesí, and everywhere he went, he searched for Marie, the young lady. He

found many girls named Marie in Bohemia. Altogether forty-nine thousand, nine hundred eighty, but none of them was expecting a letter from a driver named Frankie. Some of them, it's true, were indeed awaiting a letter from a driver, but his name wasn't Frankie but Tony or Ladie or Wenceslas, Joseph or Jarolím or else Alois or Florian and Erazim, just not Frankie. Then there were other girls by the name of Marie who were indeed expecting a letter from someone called Frankie though not from a driver, but a locksmith or a handyman, a joiner or a conductor, or a druggist as the case might be, a cabinetmaker, a barber or a tailor—just not a driver.

Mr. Kolbaba walked for a year and a day and still couldn't deliver the letter to the right Miss Marie. During this year and a day he had learned a great deal: he saw villages and towns, fields and woods, sunrises and sunsets, the return of skylarks and the coming of spring, sowing and harvest, mushrooms in the woods and ripening plums in orchards, he saw hops in Žatec, vineyards around Mělník, carps in Třeboň and gingerbread in Pardubice, but when his search had gone on for a year and a day, he grew disheartened, sat down by the roadside, and said to himself, "It's hopeless, I guess. I may not find Miss Marie, after all."

Mr. Kolbaba was heartbroken and on the verge of crying. He felt sorry for Miss Marie who hadn't received the letter from her young man who loved her more than even himself; and he felt sorry for himself, for having gone to so much trouble, having plodded through rain, in heat, in foul weather, in storms, and under stress, and all in vain.

As he was brooding by the roadside, he noticed a car approaching down the road. The car was moving slowly, I'd say about four miles an hour, and Mr. Kolbaba thought, "Some old jalopy, this one, a clunker that barely budges." But when it came closer, holy smoke! what a gorgeous eight-cylinder Bugatti it was, with a desolate-looking driver in black sitting behind the wheel, and a gentleman in black in the back.

When the sad gentleman in black noticed the lonely Mr. Kolbaba at the roadside, he ordered the car to stop, and said, "Get in, mailman, I'll give you a lift part of the way."

Mr. Kolbaba was pleased, for after all that long trudging his legs were worn out. He sat down beside the mournful gentleman in black, and the car began to inch along slowly and haplessly.

After they had gone about two miles, Mr. Kolbaba queried, "Would it be too bold to presume that the gentleman is on his way to a funeral?"

"We are not," the sorrowful man said in a hollow voice. "And what would make you think we were going to a funeral?"

"Well," said Mr. Kolbaba, "you seem so sad."

"I am so sad," the man said in a sepulchral voice, "because my car goes so slowly and sadly."

"I see," said Mr. Kolbaba. "And why does this gorgeous Bugatti go so slowly and sadly with you?"

"Because it's driven by a grieving driver," the man in black said mournfully.

"I see," said Mr. Kolbaba. "Would you permit me to inquire, your worship, why your driver is so sad?"

"He never received an answer to the letter he mailed a year and a day ago," replied the gentleman in black. "You see, he wrote to his beloved and she never answered. So, now he believes that she doesn't love him any longer."

Upon hearing this, Mr. Kolbaba burst out, "Allow me to inquire. Would your driver's name be Frankie, by any chance?"

"Well, his name is Frank Svoboda," answered the sad gentleman.

"And could the young lady's name be Marie?" Mr. Kolbaba proceeded.

Now the crestfallen driver broke in, and said with a plaintive sigh, "Miss Marie Novák is the name of that faithless woman who has forgotten my love."

"Well, I'll be..," exclaimed Mr. Kolbaba joyfully. "My dear fellow, so you are that trombone, that ramble-bumble, that cuckoo, that trumpet, that screwball, that booby noodle, that poppyseed bean, that clumsy bungler, that blackhead, that swab, that dunderhead, that flummox, that lettuce, that flibbertigibbet, that dolt, saphead, half-wit, crackbrained dude, that stuffed cucumber, that nincompoop, that deadwood, that ninny, that egg plum, that simpleton, that joker, that rattlebrain, that scatter-brain who dropped that letter in the mailbox without a stamp, and without any address to boot! Holy smoke! Am I happy to have the honor of making your acquaintance! How could Miss Marie have written back to you when she never received that letter of yours, pray tell?"

"What? Where? Where is my letter?" Frankie the driver cried.

"Just so you know, if you tell me where your Miss Marie lives, your letter will go straight to her. Would you believe that I've been carrying that letter in my bag for a year and a day, looking all over the world for the real Miss Marie? Now come on my friend, hurry up, lickety-split, on the double, and give me that address at once! I'll go to her and will personally deliver your letter."

"You won't go anywhere," said the gentleman. "I'll take you there with me. Frankie, give it some gas, and let's go!"

As he spoke, Frankie stepped on the gas, the car jerked forward and hurtled down the road full steam, twenty, thirty, forty miles an hour, then fifty, sixty, seventy, and faster all the time until the motor sang, howled, gloated and roared out of sheer joy. The gentleman in black had to grip his hat with both hands to keep it from blowing away; Mr. Kolbaba clutched the seat with both hands; and Frankie yelled, "She's moving now! How about it, boss? One hundred miles an hour! Full speed! Right off into the air! Look, boss, where did the road go? We've grown wings, sir! Wow!"

As they flew for a while at one hundred three miles an hour, a nice white village sprouted before them—

by golly, if it wasn't Libňatov!—and Frankie said, "Sir, I fancy we've arrived."

"Well, then stop!" said the gentleman in black, and the car swooped down to the ground, just outside the village. "Doesn't this Bugatti drive beautifully?" the gentleman gloated. "Now, would you deliver the letter to Miss Marie, Mr. Kolbaba?"

"Considering it has eight spelling mistakes, it just may be better if Frankie himself told Miss Marie what's written inside."

"How could I, for crying out loud?" Frankie objected. "I'm ashamed to let her see me. Anyway," he added sadly, "after all this time, she may have forgotten me altogether. She may not love me any longer. Look, Mr. Kolbaba, she lives in that little cottage over there, the one with windows as sparkling as spring water."

"I'm on my way," said Mr. Kolbaba, whistling a happy little postilion tune into his closed fist, and putting his best foot forward, as he strode toward the little cottage. There at the window sat a pale maiden, sewing a frock for herself.

"Bless you, Miss Marie," cried out Mr. Kolbaba. "Will this be a wedding gown?"

"No," answered Miss Marie gravely, "it's a shroud for my coffin."

"Dear me!" said Mr. Kolbaba with compassion. "Good heavens! Don't say things are that bad! My dear, you aren't ailing, are you?"

"No, I'm not," sighed Miss Marie, "but my heart's breaking with sorrow," and she placed her hand over her heart.

"Good Lord! Wait!" cried Mr. Kolbaba, "don't let it break yet! Would you mind telling me why your heart aches so?"

"Today it has been a year and a day," said Miss Marie softly, "one day and a year that I've been waiting for a letter that has never arrived."

"Don't let it worry you," Mr. Kolbaba said soothingly. "Look, I've been carrying a letter here, in my bag, for a year and a day because I couldn't find anyone to give it to. Now, what would you say if I gave it to you?" and with that, he handed her the letter.

215

Miss Marie blanched even more. "Sir," she said in a soft voice, "but, for all that I know, this letter may not be for me, there's no address on it!"

"Why don't you have a look," asked Mr. Kolbaba, "and if it's not for you, then you'll give it back to me. Go right ahead."

With trembling hands, Miss Marie opened the letter, and as she read it, her face brightened with elation.

"Now what about it?" asked Mr. Kolbaba. "Will you give it back to me or not?"

"I won't," sighed Miss Marie, and her eyes filled with tears of joy. "It's the letter I've been expecting for a year and a day! Dear sir, how shall I thank you? I'd love to give you something for it!"

"You owe me two crowns as a fine, since that letter wasn't properly stamped. Would you believe it, I've been running around with this letter for a year and a day so that the post office could get two crowns for the postage! Thank you kindly," he said as he received the two crowns. "You needn't bother to answer, as there's someone waiting outside." He waved to Frankie who was standing around the corner.

While Frankie was receiving his answer, Mr. Kolbaba sat down with the gentleman in black and said to him, "Dear sir, I've been running about with that letter for a year and a day, but it's all been worthwhile because of all I've seen. What a lovely and beautiful country this is, whether around Pilsen, or around Hořice, or by Tábor. Look, Frankie's coming back already. A matter like that is settled much faster in person than through a letter with no address on it, no doubt about it!"

Frankie didn't say a word, but his eyes were shining. "Shall we go, boss?" he asked.

"Yes, let's go," said the gentleman. "First, let's take Mr. Kolbaba to the post office."

Frankie jumped into the car, turned the key, disengaged the clutch, and stepped on the accelerator, and the car began to roll so smoothly and lightly as if in a dream. In a flash, the hand on the speedometer leaped to sixty.

"Doesn't she run beautifully?" said the gentleman in black with zest. "She's sailing along with spunk and zing, and with one happy driver behind her wheel!"

So they all reached the end happily, and we did too.

The
Great
Doctor's
Tale

I t has now been a very long time since Magiash the magician carried on his trade on Magus Mountain. You know, of course, that magicians are divided into good ones, known as wizards or miracle workers, and wicked ones, who are called sorcerers. Magiash fit somewhere in between. At times he was so well behaved that he wouldn't practice sorcery at all, but on other occasions he would apply his craft with such might that the skies thundered and lightning flashed. When fancy visited him, he would will it to rain rocks, and once, imagine, he even made tiny frogs fall from the sky. Say what you may, such a magician wouldn't be the most pleasant of neighbors, and even if people swore by their souls that they didn't believe in magicians they still would rather keep clear of Magus Mountain. When they claimed that the mountain was too steep, it was only an excuse— they simply wouldn't concede that they feared Magiash! Of course they wouldn't!

Now one day, Magiash sat in front of his cave just eating plums—those large, inky colored, beautifully hoarfrosted plums—while inside the cave, his underling, the freckled Vince, whose real name was Vincent the Rogue from Evilville, stood over a fire stirring magic potions made of tar, valerian, mandrake, snakeroot, knapweed, burdockroot, devilroot, grease, hell stones, hoodoo-voodoo, hoary sagebrush, goat drippings, wasp stings, rats' whiskers, tiny tomcat feet and Zanzibar seed—well, made of all such magic spices, ingredients, gallimaufry, and pestiferous weeds. Magiash kept watch on the freckled Vince as he stirred the hodgepodge, and he kept on eating the plums. However, poor Vince forgot to stir and somehow or other, the potions in the kettle got scorched,

221

burned, singed, and charred, sending forth a terrible
stench.

"You clumsy oaf!" Magiash was about to blast,
but in the rush he either confused the windpipes in his
throat, or perhaps the plum in his mouth had slipped. At
any rate he swallowed the plum with the pit, and the pit
went down the wrong way, got stuck in his throat, and
wouldn't budge—neither up nor down. So Magiash had
only time to bellow, "You cl—" and that was it, not a
sound more could he utter. He hissed and he wheezed,
sounding like steam roaring from a pot. His face turned
red, his arms waved and he coughed, but still the pit would
not budge—so firmly and thoroughly had it wedged itself
in his throat.

When Vince saw this, he became frightfully
scared, thinking his master might choke to death, and said
obligingly, "You wait here, master. I'll dash to Hronov to
fetch a doctor." Immediately he struck out at an astonish-
ing pace, straight down Magus Mountain. What a pity
there was no one to time him; no doubt he would have set
a world's record.

By the time he reached Hronov and found the
doctor he could hardly catch his breath. When, at last, he
caught it by the right end, he blurted, "Doctor, come with
me at once, straight away, I mean, presto, to Master
Magiash the magician, or he'll choke to death!"

"Did you say Magiash, the one on Magus Mountain?" mumbled the doctor. "Frankly (Lord be my witness), I can't say I feel like doing it. But if you say he needs
me, then by all means. (Do I have a choice?)" And so he
went. You know, a doctor cannot refuse help to anyone,

even if he were called to treat Villainy the robber or (Lord preserve us) the devil himself. That's the kind of job it is.

So the doctor from Hronov snatched the case in which he kept his scalpels, forceps, tongs, bandages, pills, ointments, splints for broken bones, and other such tools, and followed Vince to Magus Mountain. "I hope we make it in time," fretted the freckled Vince all the way. They trod, one two, one two, over hills and across dales, one two, one two, through marshes, one two uphill, one two downhill, when at last the freckled Vince said, "Here we are, Doctor."

"At your service, Mr. Magiash," said the doctor from Hronov. "What can I do for you? Where does it hurt?"

Instead of an answer, Magiash the magician managed only to give out a rattle. He wheezed and panted heavily, pointing to his throat where the pit was stuck.

"Aha, bit of a sore throat, I see," said the doctor from Hronov. "Well, let's have a look at it. Open your mouth very wide and say aaahhh, Mr. Magiash."

Magiash the magician pulled back his black mustache, and opened his mouth wide, but aaahhh he couldn't say, for his voice was completely lost.

"So, come on, let's say it now, aaahhh," urged the doctor encouragingly. "Don't tell me you can't . . . "

Magiash shook his head to show that indeed he couldn't.

"Oh my, oh dear," said the doctor who was a trickster and a hustler, a sly fox, full of guile, a shrewd and arch fellow who lived by his wit and alas not always by his art. "Oh my, oh dear, it's very bad with you, Mr. Magiash, if you can't say aaahhh. I don't know, I don't know," he said, and began to examine Magiash. Tip-tap here, rap-tap there, he took his pulse, he checked his tongue, peered under his eyelids, beamed a light with a small mirror into Magiash's ears and nose, all the while murmuring words in Latin. And when the thorough checkup was over, his face grew extremely grave and he said, "Mr. Magiash, this is serious business. Nothing short of an emergency surgery will do. We'll need to proceed at once. But such a surgery I cannot and must not undertake on my own. To that end, I shall need some assistance. When you are ready, you will have to send for my colleagues, doctors in Úpice, Kostelec, and Hořičky, and when they get here we'll have a doctors' meeting, or consultation. Only after a mature deliberation would we undertake the requisite medical intervention, operation operandi, as we doctors call it. Think it over, Mr. Magiash, and if you accept my suggestion, send a fast courier to fetch my highly esteemed and learned colleagues."

Did Magiash have a choice? He nodded at the freckled Vince. Vince stamped his feet three times to warm up for the race and in a flash scurried down Magus Mountain. First to Hořičky, then to Úpice, and lastly to Kostelec. For the time being, let him run!

The Suleiman Princess

While the freckled Vince trotted and trailed first to
Hořičky, then to Úpice, and lastly to Kostelec to fetch the
doctors, our doctor from Hronov stayed with Magiash to
keep an eye on him and to make sure that he did not suffo-
cate. To help pass the time, he lit a cigarette and puffed in
silence.

When time began to drag, he cleared his throat
and went on puffing. Then, to shorten the long wait, he
yawned three times, and winked. After a while, he uttered,
"Ah, well." About half an hour later, he stretched and
said, "Now then." And after another half an hour passed,
he added, "How about a game of cards while we wait, Mr.
Magiash. You wouldn't have a deck here, would you?"

Since Magiash couldn't speak, he only shook his
head.

"You don't?" grumbled the doctor from Hronov.
"That's a pity. Wait now, what kind of magician are you
anyhow, without even a deck of cards? Listen, I once saw
a magician, he gave a performance in our inn. His name
was—wait, something like Smith or Don Bosco or
Dotardi, something like that. He played tricks with cards
that would make your eyes pop out of their sockets. Well,
what is there to say. One either knows one's business or
one doesn't."

He lit another cigarette and said, "Listen, since
you have no cards here, I'll tell you a fairy tale about the
Suleiman Princess. Time will pass faster. In case you've

heard the story before, just say so and I'll stop at once. Ting-a-ling, curtain! Let's begin.

"You know that beyond the Jay Mountains and the Sea of Sargass are the Dalaman Islands and beyond them, overgrown with a thick forest, lies the Sharivari desert, with the Gypsy capital, El Dorado. There runs a meridian and a parallel, stretched far and wide. Beyond the river, as you cross the wooden footbridge and turn left, down the path, past a willow shrub, on the other side of a burdock ditch spreads the great and powerful Sultanate of Suleiman. We have arrived. Are you following me? All right then.

"In that Sultanate of Suleiman, as the name already suggests, ruled Sultan Suleiman. Now the sultan had an only daughter—Grinalda was her name. Suddenly one day, without warning, Grinalda began to ail. With much sighing and grieving she began to pale, cough, and lose weight—she was languishing, withering away. The mere sight of her was all too pitiful. Needless to say, the sultan immediately called for his court wizards, exorcists, magicians, sorcerers, soothsayers, astrologers, quacks, witch doctors, and charlatans, but not one of them could make the princess well. In our country, we'd say that the girl suffered from anemia, pleurisy and bronchitis, but in the land of Suleiman neither the people nor medicine are advanced enough to have diseases with Latin names. Now you can well imagine how the old sultan must have despaired. 'Woe is me,' he said to himself, 'how I always wished for the girl to take charge of this flourishing sultanate business. Instead, the poor child is fading and expiring before my eyes, and I cannot help her.' Deep grief set in at the court and in all the land of Suleiman.

"It so happened that just then Mr. Lustig, a traveling salesman from Jablonec, in Bohemia, arrived at the Sultanate. When the news of the ailing princess reached him, he said, 'What your sultan ought to do is bring in a doctor from my country, I mean from Europe. There, medicine is far more advanced. Here, all you have are exorcists, herbalists, and magicians, but in my country, my dear fellows, we've got true, trained doctors.'

"When Sultan Suleiman learned of that statement, he called Mr. Lustig in, bought a string of glass beads from him for Princess Grinalda, and asked, 'Mr. Lustig, how do you, in your country, tell a real, trained doctor from a quack?'

" 'Very easily, Your Majesty,' said Mr. Lustig. 'In my country, sire, a doctor has the letters "Dr." before his name. Like Dr. Mann, for instance, or Dr. Palmer, and so on. If a man's name doesn't start with "Dr.", well, you know he isn't a real doctor. It's that simple.'

" 'Aha,' exclaimed the sultan, and generously rewarded Mr. Lustig with sultanas, the delicious raisins. Then he dispatched his emissaries to Europe in search of a doctor. Before they set off, he admonished them, 'Remember that a real and learned doctor is only one whose name begins with the letters "Dr." Don't bring back any other or I'll cut your ears off, and your heads as well. Now off with you!'

"If I were to tell you, Mr. Magiash, all those envoys endured and lived through, it would be a very long fairy tale. In the end, after many, many hardships, those

envoys finally reached Europe and set about to search for a doctor for Princess Grinalda.

"Thus, the procession of the Suleiman emissaries, those huge Mameluks with turbans on their heads and whiskers as thick and as long as horsetails, began its journey through a black forest. They went on and on until they met an elderly man with an ax and a saw on his shoulder.

" 'May God bless you,' spoke the old grandpa.

" 'You, too,' said the envoys. 'What's your trade, if we may ask, old man?'

" 'Oh, well, what difference does it make?' said the old fellow. "But thanks for asking, anyhow. An ordinary drudge-trudge I am, nothing much, a lumberjack logger. Drake is the name.'

"The heathens pricked up their ears and said, 'Well, sir, that certainly does make a difference. If you are indeed Dr. Ake, as you claim, we request that you accompany us to the land of Suleiman, and do it swiftly. One two three, double-quick. Our Sultan Suleiman sends his regards and respectfully asks for your presence at his court. But should you hesitate, or perhaps balk, we will drag you there by force, and that Your Worship would not wish, for sure.'

" 'You don't say,' the man wondered, 'and what would this Mr. Sultan need from me?'

" 'He's got a job for you,' answered the emissaries.

" 'Now if that's the case, I'll gladly go,' agreed the logger. 'Wouldn't you know, I've just been looking for a job. And, let me tell you, when it comes to working hard, I'm driven like a dragon.'

"The envoys winked at each other and said, 'Well, that certainly comes in handy, your honor.'

" 'Now wait a moment!' exclaimed the lumberjack. 'First, before I go anywhere, I need to know how much this Mr. Sultan will pay me for my labor. I may be a drudge, but I certainly am not a drivel, nor a drool, and I hope that that sultan of yours isn't a drowsy drone.'

" 'It truly doesn't matter,' the Suleiman envoys answered courteously, 'that you aren't Dr. Ivel. Dr. Ake is just as welcome; and as to our master, Sultan Suleiman, he isn't Dr. One, he's just an ordinary ruler and tyrant.'

" 'Sounds fine,' said the lumberjack. 'And when it comes to food, let me tell you again, I eat like a dragon, and I drink like a dromedary. Know what I mean?'

" 'We shall do everything to satisfy you, esteemed master,' the Suleimans reassured him.

"Thus, with great pomp and great esteem, they conducted the woodcutter to their ship, and then they sailed away to the land of Suleiman. When they disembarked, the sultan quickly clambered to his throne and summoned the party to him. The emissaries knelt low before him and the oldest, with the fullest and longest mustache, spoke.

" 'Our most venerable master and ruler, knight of all the faithful, Sultan Suleiman! At your noble order, we departed for the faraway island called Europe to find the most illustrious, the most reputable, and the most famous doctor for Princess Grinalda. Here he is, Your Majesty. The most esteemed and the world-renowned Dr. Ake. And what a doctor he is! Let us just say that he works like Dr. Udge, eats like Dr. Agon, drinks like Dr. Omedary and these, you know, are all famous and illustrious doctors, whence it follows that we have come across the right man and . . . well, hm . . . That's about it.'

" 'I welcome you, Dr. Ake,' said Sultan Suleiman. 'And now, I beg you to have a look at Princess Grinalda.'

" 'Sure, why not?' thought the lumberjack. The sultan personally led him into a dim, shaded chamber, adorned with the most exquisite carpets, pillows, and cushions upon which rested Princess Grinalda, dozing and looking as wan as if she were made of wax.

" 'My, oh my,' the lumberjack said with sympathy. 'That girl of yours, Mr. Sultan, I'd say, she looks a bit seedy.'

" 'Yes, that she does,' sighed the sultan.

" 'A bit faded,' the lumberjack went on, 'like a shriveled little bit of . . . well . . . '

" 'That's just it,' the sultan nodded sorrowfully, 'not even a morsel will she swallow.'

" 'Thin as a reed,' said the old man, 'like a wisp of straw. And her color's gone, Mr. Sultan. I'd say that the maiden's in a bad way. She's ill.'

" 'Forsooth she's ill," the crestfallen sultan exclaimed, "that is why I sent for you, to restore her to health. You are Dr. Ake, or . . . '

" 'Me?' exclaimed the lumberjack, dumbfounded. 'Dear God! How in the world shall I make her well?'

" 'That, I'd say, is *your* problem,' answered the sultan in a foreboding voice. 'That's the sole reason for your being here! Now you know! Just heed my words. If you fail to cure my daughter, your head will roll and you'll be past praying for.'

" 'But that's impossible,' the lumberjack protested, but Suleiman cut him off.

" 'Hold on there,' he snapped grimly. 'I've got no time to waste. I must rule. Now, get moving and show us what you can do!' And he settled himself on his throne and ruled.

" 'A fine calamity I've been saddled with,' the lumberjack thought when he found himself alone. 'To cure a princess! How should I know what to do? A fine mess, this one. Good gracious! What am I to do? If I don't cure that damsel, they'll chop my top off. If this weren't in a fairy tale, I'd say it's against the rules to hack off a fellow's noodle for no good reason. It's an act of the devil that got me into a fairy tale, for sure. In real life, nothing like this would happen to me! Now how am I to get out of this mess? That's what I'd like to find out!'

"Thinking these thoughts and still graver ones, the poor old man sat down by the front wall of the sultan's palace and sighed. 'Where, pray tell, did they get the blasted idea that I should practice medicine here? If they only asked me to chop down a tree . . . that one here, or the one over there, I'd have shown them how it was done till the chips would fly! Talking about trees . . . why, this place could use some chopping. Looks like a rain forest. The sun can't even get into the parlor. This palace of theirs must be rotten with mold, mildew, mustiness and earwigs! Just you wait! Let me show them what a job I can do!'

"He flung off his coat, spat into his palms, seized his ax and saw, and began to fell the trees that grew around the sultan's palace. They weren't pear trees or apple trees, or walnut trees—as they are in our gardens. These were palm trees, oleanders, coconut trees, dracaenas, lantanas, ficuses and mahogany trees, and other such exotic plants—trees reaching to the heavens. You wouldn't have believed your eyes, Mr. Magiash, how our lumberjack attacked those trees! By the midday chime, a wide clearing lay open round the palace. Then the old man wiped the sweat from his brow with his sleeve, took a chunk of black bread and cheese out of his pocket, and began to eat.

"Princess Grinalda had been asleep in her murky bower. With the clamor of the woodcutter's ax and saw beneath her window, she slept better than ever before. Only when the lumberjack stopped chopping and perched himself snugly on a heap of lumber to chomp on the bread and cheese did the silence awaken her.

"She opened her eyes and marveled at the strange light invading her chamber. For the first time in her life the sun, in its full splendor, filled the dim room with its heavenly light. The flood of light nearly blinded her, and the pungent and wonderful scent of freshly cut wood came in through the window. With delight, she took a long, deep breath. With that fragrance another floated in. What was it? What else that she couldn't make out smelled so delicious? She rose to have a look. Behold, instead of dank shade, she saw a glade glowing in the midday sun, and sitting in the clearing was an old man, relishing something dark and something white. That was it! That's what smelled so good. You know, somebody else's lunch always smells most alluring.

"The princess couldn't bear it any longer. The smell drove her down the stairs to the front wall of the palace. Nearer and nearer to the old fellow she moved, just to have a peek at the goodies he was munching.

" 'Ah, the princess,' said the lumberjack with his mouth full. 'You wouldn't care for bread and cheese, would you?'

"The princess blushed and twitched. She was too bashful to admit that she would love some.

" 'Here, have a bite anyhow,' said the lumberjack and with his jackknife cut off a thick slice for her.

"The princess cast a furtive glance around to make sure no one was looking. 'Thanks,' she blurted, nibbled the bread, and said, 'Hmmm, delicious!' Now I beg you, just bread and cheese! But you must know that a princess would never get a chance to taste that in all her life.

"Just then, Sultan Suleiman looked out the window. He couldn't believe his eyes. The damp shade was gone and in its place a glade was glowing in the midday sun, and right there on a pile of lumber sat the princess. Her mouth was stuffed full, and a cheese mustache covered her face from ear to ear as she wolfed down the food with more relish than ever before.

" 'Glory be!' exclaimed the Sultan with relief. 'They did bring my girl the right, learned doctor after all!'

"And from that time on, Mr. Magiash, the princess began gaining strength, her cheeks turned pink, and she ate like a she-wolf. Such is the effect of light, air, and sunshine, you know. I am telling you all this because you too live in a cavern where sun doesn't shine and which a breeze cannot touch. And that, Mr. Magiash, isn't healthy. Well, that is, in a sense, what I wanted to tell you."

* * *

As the doctor from Hronov was about to conclude his tale of the Suleiman Princess, the freckled Vince flew in, and with him, the doctors from Hořičky, Úpice, and Kostelec. "Here they are," panted Vince from afar. "Whew! I ran myself out of breath!"

"Welcome, my friends," said the doctor from Hronov. "Let me introduce you to our patient, Mr. Magiash, the warlock. His condition is most serious, but you would have noticed that at first glance. The patient indicates that he has swallowed a plum, a prune, or a pit. In my humble opinion, I diagnose his condition as acute prunitis."

"Hmmm," muttered the doctor from Hořičky. "Judging by the symptoms, it's a case of choking plumitis."

"I wouldn't wish to disagree with my esteemed colleagues," noted the Kostelec doctor, "however, all signs suggest stonepititis of the pharynx."

"Gentlemen," interrupted the doctor from Úpice, "I respectfully submit that we agree on a single diagnosis: acute prunoplumryx stonepititis."

"Congratulations, Mr. Magiash," said the doctor from Hořičky. "You have contracted a most rare and perilous disease."

"An interesting case," added the doctor from Úpice.

"I should not like to gloat though I must tell you that I've had cases that were nicer, and more interesting to boot," retorted the doctor from Kostelec. "Incidentally, have any of you heard how I cured the howling goblin, Whinny from Crow Mountain? You haven't? Then listen to this."

The Case of Whinny the Howling Goblin

"A good many years back it must be since Whinny used to dwell on Crow Mountain. You would know, of course, that he was one of the loathsomest hobgoblins ever. Imagine a fellow passing through the woods at night when, out of the dark, right behind him, he hears a neigh, a roar, a bawl, a groan, a wail, a howl, or a horrible sneer. He is seized by terror, gives a start, and scurries away at full tilt. It's a wonder he doesn't lose his wits. For years, that's what Whinny was doing—making all that mischief on Crow Mountain till people became so frightened they dreaded the place.

"One day, there came to my office an uncouth little figure of a man, his mouth stretching from one ear to the other, his throat bound with a rag of sorts, and he wheezed, hawked, coughed, croaked and grunted in a voice so husky and grating that I couldn't understand a word he said.

" 'What's the matter with you?' I asked.

" 'Somehow or other,' he wheezed, 'I became hoarse.'

" 'That I can hear. But won't you tell me who you are?' I inquired.

"At first the patient winced a little, then he blurted out quickly, 'I am, well, I'm Whinny from Crow Mountain.'

" 'Is that so,' I said. 'So you are the scoundrel, the very devil who frightens people in the woods? Well,

my dear lad, losing your voice serves you right. I should cure your lary—pharyngitis, or your windpipe, as you call it, so that you go back to whinnying in the woods and shaking people out of their wits? Do you take me for a fool? Farewell and good riddance. Croak and wheeze in peace. At least we'll be safe from you!'

"Now that goblin Whinny started pleading, 'For Lord's sake, I beg your mercy, please deliver me from this hoarseness, and I'll behave from now on. I won't frighten people—'

" 'You better not,' I said. 'You have outhowled yourself and now, you see, your voice is gone. Spreading terror in the woods, friend, that's not a job for you. The forest is a chilly place and damp too, and with your slightly delicate respiratory passages . . . I don't know, I don't know. Maybe we could do something with this hoarseness of yours but to that end, I'm afraid you'd have to retire from the scarecrow business for good, and take yourself somewhere else, far from the woods, or no one will cure you.'

"Whinny looked glum and scratched his head. 'It may be difficult, sir, to give up the scare trade. I mean, how will I make my living? All I know is how to howl and roar, but only with my voice unfizzled.'

" 'Come on, man,' I told him. 'With such phenomenal vocal powers as yours, I'd become an opera singer, an auctioneer, or possibly even a ringmaster in a circus. Here in the country, you are wasting your talents with that magnificent and impressive voice. Don't you agree? In a city you'd be able to apply yourself much better.'

" 'I've often said the same thing to myself,' Whinny confessed. 'As soon as I have my voice back, I'll give it a try. I'll do my best to find a job elsewhere.'

"So I smeared his throat with iodine, prescribed chloraseptic and permanganate to gargle with, and told him to take anginol and put hot compresses on his throat. And on Crow Mountain Whinny hasn't been heard from ever since. Indeed, he quit haunting and changed his residence. Years later, I heard of him again, but by then he was living in the big city of Balderdash where, the rumor was, he had gone into politics. He spoke at meetings with such a robust voice and with such success he became a congressman and he's making a good living in that office to this very day.

"I am telling you all this to demonstrate to Mr. Magiash how sometimes a change of air works marvels in curing certain diseases."

The Case of the Havlov Water Sprite

"Now I too, my friends, have had a fascinating case," said the doctor from Úpice. "In our town, beyond the Havlov footbridge, amid the roots of willows and alders, lived an old water sprite; Youdal was his name. He was a mopey, rude, morose grouch. Sometimes he caused floods and, occasionally, he even drowned children while they were bathing. Understandably, people loathed to see him in that river.

"One autumn day, an old man came into my office. He had on a green tailcoat, around his neck was a red kerchief, and he groaned, coughed, sneezed, snorted, sighed, sniffled, and mumbled, 'I've caught a cold, Doctor, or the cold has caught me. It hurts here, it stabs there. My back is sore, my joints are a wreck. The cough's a plague and the cold's an affliction. Please, Doc, could you write me a prescription?'

"So I examined him and said, 'It's rheumatism all right. I'll give you Elliman's linament but that alone won't do. Make sure to keep very warm and dry. Do you understand?'

" 'I do,' the old man muttered. 'However, I'm afraid the dryness and warmth will be a problem, young man. There's a hitch.'

" 'And what's that?' I inquired.

" 'You see, I'm the Havlov water sprite. How can I keep dry and warm in the waters of the river? I even wipe my nose with a waterleaf. In water I sleep and water is my bedcover. Only now, in my old age, to help me rest, I make

241

my bed with soft water instead of hard, as I used to. The way I see it, the dryness and warmth, that will be tough.'

" 'You may be right, Gramps,' I told him, 'but in those cold waters your arthritis will only worsen. Old bones need warmth, you know. And while we're at it, how old are you anyhow?'

" 'Ah well,' mumbled the water sprite. 'I'd say I've been around ever since pagan times—some thousand years or so, maybe even longer. Ah, well, it's not worth counting.'

" 'So you see at your age, Grandpa,' I told him, 'you ought to keep close to the hearth. Wait! I've got an idea! Ever heard of hot springs?'

" 'Yeah, I have, I have,' mumbled the old water sprite. 'As far as I know there aren't any around here.'

" 'Not right here,' I said, 'but there are some in Slovakia, for instance. In Teplice, Piešťany, and in other places too. Those hot springs are deep underground. Also, let me tell you that they were made especially for old water sprites who suffer from arthritis. All you need is to establish yourself in such a hot spring as a water sprite, and you'll cure your arthritis at the same time.'

" 'Hmmmm,' the old fellow mused. 'And what does such a hot-water sprite do for a living?'

" 'Not much,' I said. 'All he has to do is keep drawing the hot water from the earth's heart so it doesn't cool off, while the leftover runs on the ground. That's all.'

" 'Doesn't sound too bad,' mumbled the Havlov water sprite. 'I'll look into it. I'll be looking around for a hot spring. Thanks a lot, Doc.'

"Then, he hobbled off, leaving behind a little puddle of water on the floor.

"Now you see, my friend, that water sprite from Havlov was smart enough to recognize good advice when he heard it, and he heeded it too. He settled in Slovakia in a hot spring and he's drawing so much hot water from the middle of the earth that now there's a fountainhead of an eternal warm stream. People travel there from all around the world to take baths and cure their rheumatism.

"It would be wise, Mr. Magiash, if you too followed the example of the old water sprite and minded your doctor's advice."

The Case of the Water Nymphs

"I once had an unusual case myself," said the doctor from Hořičky. "It happened one night. I was sleeping like a log when someone tapped on my window, calling, 'Doctor! Doctor!'

"I opened the window. 'What's going on?' I asked. 'Has someone called me?'

" 'Yes,' said a sweet, anguished voice from the dark. 'Come! Come and help!'

" 'Who's there?' I asked. 'Who's that calling for me?'

" 'I, the voice of the night,' came a reply from the darkness. 'The voice of the moonlit night. Come!'

" 'Coming,' I said as if dreaming. I dressed quickly. When I stepped outside, there was no one.

"Gentlemen, I felt rather uncomfortable. 'Hello there,' I called in a low voice. 'Is anyone here? Where should I go?'

" 'Follow me, follow me,' sobbed a faint invisible voice, and I followed. I trailed the voice as if by blind impulse, through dewy meadows and a black forest. The moon shone and the world seemed frozen in a frosty beauty. Gentlemen, I know our countryside like the palm of my hand, but on that moonlit night it appeared unreal as a dream. That happens, sometimes, and when it does, we may unearth a new world in a place that is closest to us.

"After I had pursued the voice for quite some time, I said to myself, by George . . . this looks as if it could be the Valley of Ratiboř. 'This way, doctor, here,' cried the voice. The sound of it was like the sound of a ripple on a river, glittering and murmuring. There I stood, on the bank of the river Úpa, in a silvery glade under the moonlight, and in the middle of the meadow I saw a shimmering . . . a body, perhaps. Maybe just mist. I heard it sobbing softly. But then, it may have been only the humming of the water.

" 'Hush,' I said soothingly. 'Now who are you, would you tell me, and where does it hurt?'

"From the brilliant light a trembling voice answered, 'I am only a fairy, a water nymph, a wild maiden of the waters. My sisters were dancing, and I was dancing with them. Then, I don't know what happened, a moonray may have tripped me or I may have slipped on the glitter that quivers on a dewdrop. I don't know what really happened. All I know is that suddenly I was lying on the ground, I couldn't rise, and my leg was aching, aching . . . '

" 'It could be a fracture, a broken bone, I mean, and that can be set right. Now tell me, you are one of those water nymphs that dance here in the valley? I see . . . When a lad from Žernov or from Slatina happens into your presence you dance him to death, don't you? Hmmmm . . . naughty, naughty. Don't you know, little one, that it's wicked to do that? You see, this time, your romping hasn't paid off. Well, that's what you get for frolicking about so wildly.'

" 'If only you knew how my leg hurts,' groaned the little light on the glade.

" 'Sure it hurts. A fracture ought to hurt,' and I knelt down by the water nymph to nurse her broken leg.

"My dear fellows, in my practice I must have fixed hundreds and hundreds of fractures but let me tell you, treating fairies may have been the toughest job I'd ever had. Their bodies are made of nothing but beams of light and their bones are formed of so-called gamma rays—nothing your hands can grasp. They are delicate as a puff of air, lighter than light, and gauzy as mist. Try to make a thing like that straight, put it together, and bandage it, too. A hellish predicament! I tried to bandage her leg with gossamer but she squealed, 'Ouch! It cuts like a rope!' I endeavored to splint her tiny leg with a petal of an apple blossom and she burst out crying, 'Ah, it's as heavy as a stone!'

"What was I to do? In the end I peeled off only the glittering metallic sheen of the wings of a dragonfly and made it into two splints no thicker than a hairsbreadth. I divided a moonray from a dewdrop into seven colors of the rainbow and with the ray of the thinnest blue I fastened the splints to the fairy's broken limb. I toiled so hard I broke into a sweat. The full moon seemed to be scorching my back, like the sun in August. When I finished, I sat beside the fairy and said, 'You need to rest now and you mustn't move that leg of yours till the bones are joined. But listen, darling, isn't it astounding that you and your sisters still live here? Didn't you know that it has been a very long time since all the other fairies and water nymphs who used to reside in this realm have found a better place?'

" 'Where?' gasped the fairy.

" 'In America. In Hollywood. Where else?' I said. 'That's where they make movies. Didn't you know?

All they do is act and dance in the films, make money hand over fist, and the whole world watches them. What else is there to add? They live in dazzling fame. All the water nymphs, the fairies, the elves, and the water sprites, too, have gone to work in the movies, as if they had been swept away. If only you saw the dresses and jewels those nymphs have! Surely they wouldn't put on a modest garb like yours!' "

" 'But my frock was woven of the glow of the fireflies!' pleaded the water nymph.

" 'Exactly,' I said. 'That style has long gone out of fashion. This season calls for something quite different.'

" 'With a train?' the nymph inquired eagerly.

" 'That I couldn't tell you,' I said, 'that's not my line. But at least you ought to have a look at this Hollywood. You could get there via Hamburg or Le Havre. But I'd better go now. Soon it will be dawn, and if I am correct, you water nymphs are allowed to appear only at night. So farewell now. And remember the movies!'

"I never saw her again. Her shinbone must have healed nicely, I assume. What would you say if I told you that since that night, not a single water nymph or fairy was ever seen again in the Valley of Ratiboř. They all must have gone to Hollywood, to the movies. Next time you are in a movie theater, watch closely! The men and ladies on the screen seem to move, but they have no bodies. You wouldn't be able to touch them. They are made of beams of light. Now tell me, isn't it obvious that those are water nymphs? That's also the reason why in the movies, before the nymphs begin their performance, the lights are turned off. Those fairies and all the rest of the night sprites fear light and come to life only in darkness.

"Hence, it follows that ghosts and other fairy-tale characters simply aren't suited for life in our modern world. That is unless they decide to engage in a different, more reasonable line of work. Then there'd be opportunities galore!"

* * *

Good Lord, children! with all this talk, we very nearly forgot our Magiash the magician! No wonder. He couldn't jabber, in fact, he couldn't utter a single word with that pit stuck in his throat. All he could do was sweat with fear, roll his eyes and think, I wish those doctors would help me!

"All right, Mr. Magiash, the time has come," said the Kostelec doctor at last. "Let's get ready for surgery. First, we must wash our hands, because in surgery, the chief thing is cleanliness."

The four doctors began to wash their hands, first in warm water, then in pure alcohol, then in benzine, then in carbolic acid. Then they dressed in clean white coats. Children, the surgery's about to begin! If you cannot bear watching it, you'd better close your eyes!

"Vince, hold the patient's arms," ordered the doctor from Hořičky, "he musn't budge an inch!"

"Are you ready, Mr. Magiash?" asked the doctor from Úpice solemnly.

Magiash barely nodded. He felt that his courage would abandon him at any moment. It dwindled and shriveled to the point it could squeeze beneath a fingernail.

"One, two, three, now!" yelled the Hronov doctor.

The Kostelec doctor swung his arm and wacked Magiash on his back with such a thump—

—that skies rumbled as if thunder had struck, and people in faraway villages looked up to see whether a storm was brewing;

—that the earth quaked, a shaft in an abandoned mine collapsed, and the church spire swayed in the city of Náchod;

—that all over the countryside, as far as Trutnov and possibly even farther, all the pigeons flew up, startled, and all the dogs crawled, frightened, into their kennels, and all the cats sprang off the hearths;

—and that the plum stone jettisoned from Magiash's throat with such a tremendous force and speed that it flew beyond the city of Pardubice and landed in the village of Přelouč, killing a pair of oxen, and buried itself three fathoms, two yards, a foot and a half, seven spans, four and three-sixteenths inches deep in the ground.

The prune stone jettisoned first but right behind it followed, "—umsy oaf!" That was the half of the sentence that stuck in Magiash's throat when he called out to freckled Vince, "You clumsy oaf!" Those words, however, didn't fly as far. They landed right beyond the village of Josefov and broke apart an old pear tree.

Magiash unruffled his mustache and said, "I owe you thanks."

"The pleasure is ours," answered the doctors. "The surgery was a success."

"Yet," the doctor from Úpice broke in immediately, "it will take a couple of years of convalescence, Mr.

Magiash, before you rid yourself of this affliction altogether. I strongly urge a change of air and climate, just as you remember I had encouraged the water sprite from Havlov!"

"I concur," declared the doctor from Hronov. "To keep in good health, you need plenty of sunshine and fresh air, just like the Suleiman princess. I should heartily recommend a sojourn in the Sahara desert."

"I share your opinion," added the doctor from Kostelec. "The Sahara would be especially beneficial to your health, if only for the reason that no plums grow there that could seriously endanger your health."

"I join my esteemed colleagues," added the doctor from Hořičky. "And being a magician, Mr. Magiash, you could, in the desert, at least explore and reflect how to conjure moisture and harvest a crop so that people can live and work there. Wouldn't that make a most beautiful fairy tale?"

What was Magiash to do? He politely thanked the four doctors, packed up his hocus-pocus, and moved from Magus Mountain to the Sahara desert. Since that time, we have had no more sorcerers or black magicians here, and that's good. However, Magiash is still alive and well, speculating over how to conjure fields, forests, cities, and villages from the desert. Perhaps you children will live to see it.